THE DARK GRIMOIRES

ICYA & THE TWIN SOULS

MERJr.

MERJr. Books are published by
Croc Society Entertainment Publishing
ISBN: **978-0-578-17473-0**
Library of Congress Control Number: **2015920390**

MERJr.

Croc Society Entertainment
Publishing https://www.Darkgrimoires.com

Printed in the United States of America

Dedication & Thanks

"This book is dedicated to Mykail and Mychel Robinson. I want to thank the people who supported me throughout this process (Diana Treazur Harmony & Rhythm). I want to thank Eddick Moore for the brilliant artwork, along with Terrance Robinson, Wenda Andrews and Zenita Mitchell for supporting me from the beginning. I also want to thank Chris Jacobs, Tikimila Blockman and Ernest Green for their contributions. A special thanks goes out to my wife, Dreama Robinson. Without you, my dream would have remained only a dream."

This book was professionally edited by Linda Hall.

Chapters & Epilogue

Bold type within the story was used to illustrate active telepathy between characters.

Brief Character Descriptions

King O'Saka Navitazi is the ruler of Ardhi Anasa (a peaceful kingdom, full of magic and mystery). His main goal in life is to raise his children and to leave a rich and honorable legacy for them to continue.

Prince Saka Navitazi is the son of King O'Saka and the Crown Prince of Ardhi Anasa. He is a great son, but part of him is undeniably primal. He would do anything to make his father proud. His legacy is as great as anyone who has ever walked the earth.

Thundar Navitazi is a gorilla who has been raised with Prince Saka in the palace from a newborn. He and Saka are the same age. He loves the King and Saka. He would die to protect the people he loves. His destiny is intertwined with Prince Saka's legacy through magic.

Icya Sade Asasen is the brave and beautiful daughter of an evil voodoo king, but she is somehow allied with his enemies. She joins the fight for what is right using black magic and her amazing wits.

Mykail is a mysterious, homeless young boy who befriends Saka at a very young age. He is a very strange person, and even though he and Thundar become close, Thundar never trusts him completely.

Zulin Yang is the daughter of Master Yasufe Yang (a top official in the kingdom and a master of martial arts). Prince Saka and Zulin grow up together and fall deeply in love. She is very beautiful and bullheaded.

Chapter I

Treazur Lake

"Saka, we have to hurry. I cannot keep him under for much longer," said Icya as she repeatedly chanted a spell.

"Thundar, help me find something to bind this fool. We have to tie him up and lock him in this chest," said Saka.

Thundar then leaped into the trees, retrieved some strong vines and brought them to the Prince. "This will have to do," said Prince Saka. They then tied the unconscious prisoner and threw him inside an enormous chest. He was unusually tall, but big-boned, and black and shiny like a crow's beak.

"Hurry, he's waking up!" screamed Icya. Saka quickly closed the chest and locked it. Suddenly, the chest began to shake uncontrollably.

"Ahhhhh," yelled Icya, holding her head and with tears in her eyes as they rolled back in her head and veins popped out of her neck. "He's awake!" she yelled.

"Now, brother, drag him to the deepest, darkest part of the lake so that he may never rise again," said Saka. Thundar then grabbed the heavy chest with both hands, raised it over his head, jumped twenty feet in the air towards the middle of the lake and went in headfirst. The air inside of the large wooden chest pulled upwards against Thundar's descent, but he was a powerful swimmer, so he continued onward, diving deeper and deeper into the abyss. Now the entrapped prisoner was attempting to scream, but the cursed water had already begun to eat away at his skin and, eventually, nothing but his skeleton remained.

A century ago, a spell had been set upon the lake. Any human who entered would burn, as if he/she had bathed in acid. Only animals could enter. Treazur Lake was as clear as crystal, and the farther Thundar descended, the more the name of the lake revealed itself. Tiny diamonds and different colored rubies in the millions swirled in clusters amidst large schools of brightly painted, small fish. Now Thundar had come upon the bottom of the dark abyss and was tying the chest to a large smooth rock. As he tied the last knot around the giant gem, the rope was snatched out of his hand, and now the chest was shaking again, as if the corpse had come back to life. Thundar swiftly secured the chest and looked inside a small hole.

"**Saka, I wish you could see this,**" said Thundar. To his surprise, the corpse was fully restored to its former likeness and dreadfully reliving his previous horrible death.

"**Serves him right for what he did,**" said Thundar as he swam back towards the surface. Fifty feet above Thundar, at a reasonably safe distance from the lake, the Prince and Icya anxiously waited for him to submerge. "Is he okay?" asked

Icya.

"He's fine. There he is," said Prince Saka.

"Rhaaaarhh, it's done, brother," roared Thundar as he propelled fifteen feet into the air from the surface of the lake and landed two feet in front of the Prince.

"Thank Yeshua, you are safe," said Icya, fully exhausted, as she fainted into Prince Saka's arms. "Okay then," said Saka as he picked up Icya and held her in his arms like a sleeping infant.

"It is okay, brother. Go let her rest. You could use some, too. I will go make sure Father and the others make it home safely. I will be back in a couple of days," said Thundar. "Okay then, brother, I'll see you soon," replied Saka as he turned around and walked towards the palace, carrying the sleeping Icy

Chapter II

Recreational Areas

Growing up, Prince Saka was a happy, rambunctious boy who liked climbing anything he could wrap his fingers around. He learned to walk at about three years old by clinging on to Thundar, an African gorilla the same age as Prince Saka. They were inseparable, and even when Saka was in school, Thundar was close by, learning sign language or discipline training. Thundar wanted to learn. He was smart for a gorilla. Both he and his brother excelled at whatever task was put before them. The uniquely mentionable challenge that Saka's father, King O'Saka, had when it came to Saka was his temper. He seldom got upset but, when he did, it was monumental.

One day when Saka was about nine, he and Thundar were supposed to be in school but instead were in the forest having so much fun that they lost track of time. They loved the forest. Every day before studies, between studies and after classes, they would be in the forest, climbing and swinging.

This day, class just slipped their minds entirely. Addo (a young but experienced school guard) reported their absence to the King, so King O'Saka sent some men to look for them and bring them back. Three soldiers exited the kingdom gates to check the common spots where the brothers often played. One of the soldiers was fairly new, and Thundar did not know him. When the soldiers came to retrieve Saka and Thundar, they were both high up in one of the tallest trees in Africa, a rose gum tree. Initially, the soldiers did not see them.

"Thundar, look. They're so tiny from up here," whispered Saka.

"Hrrhuur," replied Thundar. Now, Thundar was enormous and full of muscles, with a beautiful, black shiny coat of hair. In human years, he was the same age as Prince Saka but, in ape years, he was close to eighteen and big for even that age. All he ate was bananas and boiled eggs, his favorites. His eyes were big and light brown, and he looked very intelligent. He always seemed to have a fresh haircut in the shape of a small mohawk.

"Watch this," whispered Saka as he dropped small sticks on the soldiers' heads.

"Ouch!" one of the men yelled, looking upward into the tall trees.

"Hahaha, are you looking for us?" asked Prince Saka

"Yes," said the soldier, holding his head while sitting on top of his horse.

"What is it? asked the Prince.

"I need you to come with us. Your father sent me to bring you to your daily classes," replied the guard.

"Aww man! I totally forgot! Come on, Thundar," said Saka."Hrrhuur," grunted Thundar, and both of them started racing down the tree so fast that the men could barely see them.

Twenty feet before Saka reached the ground, he began to slide down the bark of the tree. He and Thundar did this for fun, but the new man thought he was falling. So in an attempt to help him, the soldier hopped off his horse, dashed over to the tree, and mistakenly caused Saka to fall and hurt himself. Concerned, Thundar rushed over and pushed the soldier away from Saka and slammed the man hard into a tree.

"You damn monkey," yelled the soldier as he got up and drew his sword. The other men tried to stop him, but he got past them. He then slashed at young Thundar repeatedly and missed until Thundar tripped over Saka.

"I got you now!" yelled the soldier with a murderous look in his eyes. He swung his blade and cut Thundar in the middle of his forehead.

"Arrrrrh!" hollered Thundar. Then Saka aggressively got up, rushed the mad soldier, pinned him on the ground and began to beat him in the face uncontrollably with both hands. Blood was splattering on the trees as Saka screamed, "Die, die die!" The other soldiers saw that the soldier being beaten was now unconscious and tried to get the Prince off him. Thundar knocked both of them to the ground and stood over them, breathing heavily and baring his teeth. When Saka finally snapped out of his rage, the bloody, beaten man was having some sort of seizure.

"Let's go, brother," said Saka, crying a little.

One of the other soldiers asked the Prince, "Are you okay,my Prince?" Saka stayed silent. He and Thundar hopped on the beaten soldier's horse and headed for home. One soldier followed them, and one stayed behind.

On the way home, Saka noticed that someone was following them. Inconspicuously, Prince Saka alerted the soldier. " Look in the bushes to the right," he whispered. The soldier then went and flushed the person out from the bushes and brought them to the Prince. It was a small, eight-year-old boy in worn down clothes, with a scar on his chin. He looked very poor, homeless or both.

"Who are you, and what are you doing following us?" asked Saka while Thundar jumped down off the horse and began intensely sniffing and probing the stranger. The boy was scared and murmured a few words.

"Speak up!" yelled the soldier. "Myka, my name is Mykail,

" said the boy nervously. "Thundar, what's wrong?" asked Saka because he would not stop sniffing and tilting his head to the side like a dog when it hears a strange sound.

"I like to climb also, and you have a gorilla. He is magnificent. I didn't mean to start any trouble," said the young boy.

"Prince Saka, what do you want me to do with him?" asked the soldier.

"Let him go." "Where do you live?" asked the Prince. "I live in Nakuru Village," said the little boy. Nakuru was a small farmers' village about ten kilometers south of the palace.

"How did you get out here, and how are you getting home? asked the Prince.

"I walked," replied the boy.

"Guard, take Mykail to his village," said Saka, holding his left arm in pain.

"My Prince, you're hurt," said the soldier.

"I'm fine. I'll tell my father what happened. Go now," said Saka. The guard lifted the boy onto his horse, and they went on their way. Saka and Thundar took the beaten soldier's horse and headed home.

A little while later, Saka and Thundar reached the palace, where King O'Saka was waiting patiently in Saka's room on his bed.

"Saka, what are you doing? You were supposed to be in class, and what's wrong with your arm?" questioned the King, slightly angered.

"I am so sorry, Father. We were playing in the forest, and I forgot about class," saïd Saka, whimpering and holding his arm.

"Come here, son! What happened?" asked the King, pulling Saka by his hurt arm to test its strength and condition. Saka cringed in intense pain. "Let me see," said the King as he examined it further. Your shoulder is dislocated."

"Nurse," he yelled, looking intensely at Saka. "Now tell me exactly what happened!"

Saka told his father everything that happened while the nurse prepared his arm to be snapped back into place. The king listened to the story and, after Saka's arm was mended, he put him into bed and said goodnight to the young Prince and to Thundar. He then left the room and waited for the soldiers to return.

A few hours later, the guard who stayed behind arrived to tell the king what happened that day.

"Where is the soldier who wounded Thundar?" King O'Saka asked calmly.

"He is dead, sire," said the guard. "I made no such command," said the King, with more concern than anger in his voice.

"It was not by my hand,." said the guard, looking down slightly.

"Then who?" the king asked.

"It was Prince Saka. The man did not recover from the wounds the prince inflicted upon him," said the soldier.

"Why didn't you stop him?" yelled King O'Saka.

"The prince hopped on him fast and, when I tried to intervene, Thundar came upon me and threw me and the other guard to the floor. He would not let us pass.

At that moment, I saw that the Prince was in no danger. I did not expect the young Prince to draw blood, but he lost it and went into a rage. When he finally stopped, the soldier was in a bad state. I am so sorry, King O'Saka," said the guard, sounding exactly so.

"Okay, Kintu, so where is the body?" asked the King.

"I dumped it in Treazur Lake," he replied, seeking the King's approval.

"Good and never, ever speak of this again or you will join him in his choice of recreational areas," said King O'Saka.

Chapter III

Little Spy

(Two weeks later)

"Well, Saka's arm is better. Back to running, wrestling and sliding down trees," said King O'Saka, thinking out loud as he watched Saka and Thundar race off to the forest after class. "Kintu, have you seen or heard from the little boy Mykail since that day?" asked the King.

"No, Your Majesty," he replied. "Saka has asked about him several times. Go see if you can find him at his village. If you find him, bring him so he and Saka can play," commanded the King.

"Okay, I'll leave for the village now, Your Majesty," replied Kintu. On his way out of the palace gates, he passed by Saka and Thundar.

"See you later," shouted Saka.

"So brother, what are we going to conquer today?" asked Saka, signing to Thundar.

"Don't know," replied Thundar, shrugging his shoulders.

"I know," said a familiar voice from the bushes. Thundar quickly dashed toward the voice and flushed Mykail out. "Sorry, Thundar, didn't mean to startle you, boy," said Mykail while being severely sniffed and probed by Thundar.

"It's you again. How long have you been waiting there?" asked Saka.

"Not long," replied Mykail.

"So where do you go to have adventures?" asked the Prince.

"Oh adventures you say; well now … you are sure dressed for the occasion. Do you always dress alike?" asked Mykail.

Saka and Thundar looked at each other and then Saka replied, "Yes. Is something wrong with that?"

"No, nothing at all," said Mykail, looking away slightly embarrassed. Saka was wearing a black leather fitted vest with dark blue leather fitted short pants that came down to his thighs, and a black flap that covered his loin area. Thundar was dressed the same, and both of them carried a black satchel.

"Are you ready?" asked Mykail hastily.

"On our way then," replied the Prince. Thundar was still looking at Mykail like a confused dog.

On the way to their destination, Saka noticed that Mykail had the same clothes he had on when they had met. He also noticed that he walked with a limp. "So Mykail, do you go to school?" asked the Prince.

"Yeah, of course, my class ended already," replied Mykail.

"Oh okay then," said the Prince with one eyebrow lifted. At that moment, the forest began to get so thick that the sun stopped shining through the trees.

"Did you injure your leg?" asked Saka. "Yeah, I did," replied Mykail.

"How?" asked the Prince.

"I fell coming down that tree," replied Mykail, looking up at an enormous tree that seemed to reach the heavens.

It was wider and taller than any tree that Saka and Thundar had ever seen. It was so magnificent that both of them just stood there and looked at it in awe for ten minutes without saying, signing or grunting a single thing. Then in a flash, both of them were climbing rapidly, leaving Mykail behind watching in amazement. Higher and higher and faster and faster they climbed until both of them had disappeared into the branches, Thundar first, then Saka right after. The tree was so big that the farther they went up, the darker it got.

"Hold on, brother. Be careful. I think something is up here with us," whispered Saka. Both of them could hear all kinds of noises coming from all around them and, a little farther up the tree, something was shining that looked like two blue eyes. "Helloooo," shouted Saka, slowly climbing toward it. Thundar cautiously got closer to the object than Saka. What they found glowing way up in this tree of trees would eventually change their lives and the lives of everyone around them forever. When they finally came upon it, they discovered two amulets that produced a light that glowed without any sunlight. "Nice!" said Saka as he grabbed the amulets and attached them to a gold chain around his neck. "Ahhhhr, it hurts," he screamed as he began to faint.

Luckily, Thundar caught him, put him on his back and began to descend quickly down the tree. Halfway down, Saka's chain got tangled in a branch, and both amulets fell.When they finally got to the ground, Mykail was gone, but thankfully Saka regained consciousness and the amulets lay at the base of the tree. He grabbed them and put them in his satchel, and they began walking home.

Chapter IV

Koulev Senkyem

On the way home, Saka seemed to be deep in thought, every so often glancing down at his satchel. When they reached the palace, King O'Saka and the General of the Ardhi Anasaian Army, General Nakatu, were talking in the courtyard.

"I believe it is time for Saka to begin combat training," King O'Saka said to Nakatu.

"That is an excellent idea, sire," he replied.

"I will reserve Master Yasufe to train him in hand-to-hand combat and the ways of the sword. These lessons will give him the extra discipline he requires." Now, the King saw Saka and Thundar and said, "Come here, you two. Let's talk."

Saka said excitedly, "Father, I want to show you something." As he pulled the talismans out of his satchel, King O'Saka instantly noticed what they were and asked his son where he found it. Saka told him the story but left out Mykail all together.

"Are both of you okay?" asked the King.

"I'm fine," replied the Prince.

"Saka, please express to Thundar, in sign, my appreciation for his actions in the forest that more than likely saved your life," said the King.

Saka did what he was told. "He said that I am his brother and he would die for me," Saka said.

"I believe him," King O'Saka said. "Saka, you have to be more careful. I have to worry about you every time you leave the palace," said the King.

"I will, Father," replied Saka.

"Now Saka, I need you to listen. I have seen something like this before. These are very dangerous, and I need you to give them to me for safekeeping," said the King, bending down to one knee in front of Saka.

"But Father," said Saka. "I tell you what, we will make a trade," said the King, reaching to his side and drawing a magnificent sword with a black and golden handle.

"Wow! Thanks, Father," said Saka, excitedly grabbing the sword.

"Whoa son, be careful. I had it made just for you, and it is very sharp. So do we have a deal?" he asked.

"Deal," replied Saka.

"You begin combat training tomorrow," said the King.

Later on, after nightfall, King O'Saka retired to his study and closely examined the amulets. Both were identical (a silver circle with one large blue stone in the center, four snake patterns going around it with a place for one small gem in between each snake pattern).

King O'Saka heard someone coming. "Sire, may I enter?" asked General Nakatu. "Come in, old friend," replied the King. "What are they?" asked Nakatu.

"These are the Koulev Senkyem, the five snake amulets. Supposedly, there are but four in existence. The great JuJu King, Pouvwa Bondye, told my father and my father told me that these amulets give the wearers the ability to communicate telepathically. My father spoke of these in great detail. I also saw drawings of these same amulets in the book of Dark Grimoires, but they are a lot older than the book.

They date back to the original man and woman. The medallion and stones inside of them gave the wearers complete power of the earth, and everything on it. There were two then. But because of sin, God took the gifts away from them and he divided the power of each medallion in half, making four all together. They were spread in pairs across the earth, but most of the earth was one big continent called Ethiopia. Saka and Thundar have stumbled on the most important find in history. In the Dark Grimoires, it is written that the war for the earth will be fought between the owners of the pairs of medallions, good vs evil" said the King.

"I see now what needs to be done. I had forgotten something very strange that I had seen as a boy inside the Dark Grimoires," said the King, scratching his chin with a wild look in his eyes.

"What is it, sire?" asked the general.

"Under the drawing of the Koulev Senkyem there was another drawing. It was the image of an infant boy and infant gorilla siting back to back, both wearing crowns. Finding both of these medallions is not by chance. It was fate, and this is what we have to do. Up until the Prince"s 18th birthday, Thundar and I will test the medallions thoroughly and, if everything goes smoothly with no harm coming to either of us, I will give the other medallion to Saka.

I want you to use the amulets to train Thundar in combat and the use of the spear. We will get the blacksmith to construct a spear of iron for him. Everything is done in secret of course. You will train him at the same time his other classes would have been. The amulet is supposed to open up a part of the mind that heightens intelligence, even in animals. I want you to teach Thundar everything you know. He already possesses an uncanny love for Saka that even rivals my own. Their bond is closer than any sibling bond I've ever seen."

"Once when they were three years old,

Thundar was wandering around the palace while everyone was asleep. He ended up in this very room. He climbed to the top of that bookshelf, fell and broke his leg. At the same time, Saka woke up out of his sleep, screaming and holding the same leg that Thundar broke," said the King.

" I remember, sire. I found Thundar and brought him to you," said Nakatu.

"Oh yeah, that's right," said the King, looking more serious. "Saka is the sole heir to the throne, and I feel certain evil brewing. My old friend Congion is up to something. We must to prepare the prince in any and every way possible. These medallions are a blessing in disguise," said King O'Saka.

Chapter V

The Link

The next morning, the King met Prince Saka coming out of his first class and walked him to the next one. On the way, he asked his son if he could hang out with Thundar while he was in training. "Of course, Father," replied Saka.

"Well here you are son. Good morning, Master Yasufe," said the King.

"Good morning, sire," he replied.

"Okay then, I'll leave you to it, son, Master Yasufe," said King O'Saka, saying goodbye.

"Bye, Father. See you after class, brother," yelled Saka as he saw Thundar coming from his first class.

"Hey, Thundar, come here son. Let's go to my study and experiment for a while," said the King.

When they arrived at the study, King O'Saka was anxious but also reluctant to test the amulets. He then said a short prayer and put the first amulet around his neck. He stood there for a little while and nothing happened. But when he put the other talisman around Thundar's neck, both of them dropped to their knees. Their eyes lit up like the sun, and a gust of wind blew through so strong that it strummed some eerie notes on a long-neck lute sitting in the corner. For five minutes, neither of them could move.

When they were finally able to move, King O'Saka said in his mind, **"Thundar, can you hear me?"** Thundar stood there with a confused, scared look on his face and replied, **"Yes!"**

"Do you understand everything I am saying?" asked the king.

"Yes, but Father how is this possible?" he asked.

"The talisman gives us the power to communicate with each other mentally and enhances our learning capabilities. The sign lessons and the fact that you have been around humans your whole life hearing us converse has contributed to your complete coherence. I was so afraid to have you join me in testing the amulets, but I asked myself, if I would have asked you to make the choice between you and Saka, the choice would have been the same. Am I correct?" asked the King.

"Yes, Father," replied a wide-eyed Thundar.

"Okay then! In the next few days, you will begin your combat training. Nakatu will be your guide. You will learn fast, so follow him closely. We will also work together and learn together to perfect the link. In a few years, I will give the amulets to you and Saka," explained the King.

"Thank you, Father," said Thundar, almost in tears.

"No, my son. Thank you for being a loving and loyal brother to Saka. I do not love you like a son. I love you because you are my son. Now Thundar, every time I place that talisman on your neck, no one is to remove it except for me. Is that understood?" asked the King.

"Yes, I understand," replied Thundar.

"Okay, that's enough for today. Let's see if we remember in detail our conversation after the talisman is removed," said the King.

As the King removed the talisman from Thundar's neck, he heard Thundar saying, "Thank you, Father ... thank you, Father" until the effects of the talisman completely faded. Then all of the light was sucked out the room, and a strong gust of wind again blew through, strumming the lute, and both of them were brought to their knees.

"Thundar, are you okay? Can you understand me? Do you remember what we spoke about?" asked King O'Saka.

At first, Thundar stood there in a daze, with his eyes bucked wide open for a second. Then he gradually nodded his head up and down. "Here is a book called (The Art of War). Open it," demanded the King. "Can you read it?" he asked.

Thundar nodded yes.

"This will be the first book you read. It is yours, but I'll keep it here," said the King. "Now go meet Saka and say nothing of this as of now. Meet me here the same time tomorrow."

For the next two months, the King and Thundar tested the amulets. Thundar journeyed farther and farther into the forest each day. He learned new pathways and hidden routes on land and under water. He learned how to swim fluently in just one day. Thundar could stay submerged under water for twenty minutes now with no problem. The amulets' effects on the brain were extraordinary. His senses like sight and smell, which were already strong, were incredibly powerful now.

At the end of the second month of training with the amulets, on another beautiful sunny day, King O'Saka told Thundar to take a horse so he could go farther this time, and he asked him, "Thundar, why do you always go in the same direction?"

Thundar replied, "At first it was because it was familiar, but now I feel there is something pulling me in this direction. I do not know what it is, Father. The farther I go south, the stronger I feel it."

"What does it feel like?" asked the King.

"Right now, I can hear a humming in my right ear and the right side of my head feels warm. It doesn't hurt," replied Thundar.

"Wow, that's interesting," said the King. "I also hear the same humming in my head. Well, don't let that worry you. Whatever it is will reveal itself when the time is right. Just be careful out there," said King O'Saka.

"Yes, Father, I will," answered Thundar. "Father, can you tell me the story of how you found me again if it's not too painful? I want to hear it while I have the amulet on," said Thundar.

"No, it's okay, I'll tell you again," replied the King. So while Thundar rode the horse like the whipping wind, the King told him the story of how he became part of the royal family.

Chapter VI

A Mother's Love

"I can remember it so clearly now," said King O'Saka. "It was on a day similar to this one. Nidera was 8 1/2 months pregnant. When I woke up that morning, she was already awake and had been watching me sleep for a while I guess. I asked her if she was okay. She assured me everything was fine. She was so beautiful. The most beautiful, loving woman you could ever imagine. It's true that when a woman is pregnant, she has a special glow. Her shimmer rivaled the moon itself on her gloomiest day. She would have been the greatest mother."

"Anyway we got up, got ready, and I remember asking her why she had so much luggage. It was ridiculous. When we got outside, Zolatar and Volaris were waiting but, in hindsight, they were not excited like their usual selves. (Zolatar and Volaris were two of the last Terroraptors, said to be the most feared and fierce animals on the planet. Zolatar the male and Volaris the female weighed over two thousand pounds each. They were hundreds of years old but moved and played around like teenagers. The way to tell them apart was the thickness of the long, black, shiny horns that stretched out three feet from each of their heads. Zolatar's horn was much thicker. They were extremely powerful and at top speed could run three times faster than a cheetah. They were a gift from Pouvwa Bondye and were King O'Saka's most prized possessions.) I noticed it then, but I was more focused on the Queen and the road ahead. Something was wrong with both of them.

Congion was there. At the time, he was our chief witch doctor, and he was to ride in the carriage in front of Nidera and me in case of any complications. I had told him he could ride with us, but he insisted we ride alone because maybe we could have intercourse. He said that at this time in the pregnancy, intercourse would make it easier for Nidera to deliver. He was being serious and funny at the same time. He and I grew up together. We had been best friends from infancy.

Pouvwa Bondye served my father as his chief adviser and was lead in all things dealing with voodoo and magic. He and his wife adopted Congion because no matter what they tried, they could not have children. Now I'm thinking maybe it was him who was incapable of producing, because she wasn't his first wife and he never had any kids besides Congion.

Well, we were on our way to Borelsand, the holy land, the one place fit for the birth of the Prince. Fifty men on horseback accompanied us, and we were moving at a quick but steady pace.

The carriage in which we traveled had been recently built specifically for this trip. It was extravagant and big enough for four people, with two beds. It was full to capacity with luxuries, food and Nidera's belongings. It even doubled as a boat and had a toilet inside. It would have probably taken eight horses to pull it, yet a mere two master rhino were more than enough to perform the task.

It was our third day of travel on a five-day trip. We were deep into the Karura Forest, crossing over the Victoria River. As soon as we got to other side, it began to rain. Then in the middle of the day, it turned pitch-black and a bone-cracking cold descended on the forest. I say that it went from hot to freezing in seconds and from day to night. Nidera was frightened. Never in my day had I seen a change in the weather happen so fast. As soon as the rain started coming down hard, I ordered everyone to stop and told Congion to come ride with us. He came, but he was in the corner chanting the whole time. At the time, I thought the chants were to our benefit. So after I got my Nidera to calm down, I looked out of the window, then immediately as I said to Nidera, "Everything is going to be fine," lightning struck this big tree at the top of a tall hill to the right of us. It then struck a second time at the base of the tree. The third time it struck, the tree tilted over toward us and started falling. The driver attempted to move us out of its path, but the tree caused a mudslide that almost killed us all. Then a huge wall of mud crashed into the carriage with so much force that we slammed against the walls several times until my dear Nidera was forced from my grip.

At the same time, my eyes passed over Congion pressed up against the wall but, when I think about it, he stuck to or blended in with it. When the carriage finally stopped sliding, it was flipped over on its side and all the way covered in mud. I could feel my ribs were broken as I yelled out to the Queen but got no reply. I could hear someone moving around, but it turned out to be Congion. I got up to look for her still, calling out to her. It was pitch- black inside the carriage, and I was dazed. Thank Yeshua, I could feel the carriage moving. It was my two friends Zolatar and Volaris pushing us out from under the mud. Now, some sunlight was beaming through, and I could see her. A long branch had gone through the right side of her stomach and pinned her to the wall. Congion and I ran to her and got her down. I was so scared because she was dying in my arms and I could not do anything about it, so in a panic I grabbed my sword, put it to Congion's neck and told him to save her, for the life he'd truly save would be his own.

He started to say something but, before he got it out, Nidera, gargling in her blood, said, "It's too late for me. Please, my love, save our child." I knew I had to act swiftly so I kissed her for the last time and as became lifeless,

I pierced her stomach with the tip of my sword. Gently, I reached inside her and pulled Saka out of the cut that I made, but he was without life.

Congion saw that Saka was stillborn, so with no delay he opened his large book of spells and started chanting ancient words that again abruptly brought forth a silence and bone-numbing cold, then the clouds swallowed up the sun. I could not breathe this time, so I opened the half-broken door to the carriage to get some air and to maybe help Saka. As soon as I opened the door, I saw a female gorilla, lying slain from the mudslide. Clinched in her bosom were her twin infant boys. The smaller of the gorilla twins was gasping for air and, as soon as he stopped breathing, I heard the most wonderful sound I had ever heard in my life. Loud cries from the newborn Prince echoed through forest like a lion's majestic roar.

There is no way to express the amount of joy I felt at that moment, but the amount of pain soon returned with equal force for as I glanced back toward the corpse of my beloved Nidera, my heart shattered into pieces.

At this time, I did not understand what Congion had done, but now after acquiring knowledge using the amulets' power, I realized the truth.

Congion used a gelede ritual that caused the fleeing soul of the stillborn Prince to seek out another young soul and steal its life essence. The ritual pulled the life from your small gorilla brother and blessed Saka with his essence. So, in essence, you and Saka are eternally connected, with a bond forged by magic.

"Praise Yeshua," said Thundar, as he raced on. "Praise you, Father!"

Shortly after, while preparing the Queen for the journey home, I remembered that you were still clinched in your mother's bosom. So I went to you, reached down and pulled you from her caring hand. And with you in one arm and Prince Saka in the other, I said to you, "It's okay fella, you lost one brother, but now you have another one." As long as I have lived, I have never seen closeness like that of you and your brother. Even my brother and I did not share the bond that you and Saka have shown growing up together. Now I know why, and now you know.

On the way home, I recalled everything that had happened, and I planned to question Congion as soon as we got home, but he was not in his carriage when we arrived. I never saw him or Yewande (his apprentice and mother of two of his children) ever again. Elder Sheshon child was taken also," said the King.

But why would Congion want to hurt you or the Queen?" asked Thundar.

"I truly believe he blamed me for his wife's death in some way. On many occasions, he asked and practically begged me to give him the Dark Grimoires, but I had sworn not to let anyone get their hands on it because the use of its spells can simply end in eternal death. He thought one of the spells could cure his wife and, even after she died, he wanted to use it to bring her back to life. We argued many times over this. He told me that I did not know how it felt to lose a wife and that if I had felt that pain, I would use the forbidden ritual without hesitation. He was wrong. I loved and still love Nidera with all my heart and soul, but I will not dishonor her by bringing her back to this wicked place. Well, go ahead and turn around, that is enough for today," said King O'Saka.

"Okay, Father," said Thundar, and he returned home shortly.

Chapter VII

Prying Eyes

Every day after lessons, Saka and Thundar still went on their adventures, and Mykail would always pop up. The three eventually became close, but Thundar always seemed to sense something strange from Mykail. One day, close to the year after Thundar began his training with General Nakatu, Saka invited Mykail to the palace. He agreed to visit the next day on the condition that he could spend the night because his parents did not want him to be out in the woods at a late hour. Saka considered the request reasonable and asked his father. King O'Saka said yes, and the next morning there were no classes, so Saka and Mykail met at the palace gates bright and early.

"So what did your father say?" asked Mykail with a big smile on his face.

"He said hell no," replied Saka with a mean scowl that soon turned into a huge smile. "I'm just kidding. Come on in, my friend," said Saka. As soon as they entered the palace, Mykail's jaw dropped.

"Holy moly, everything is so beautiful," whispered Mykail.

"Beautiful," said Prince Saka, chuckling and looking at Thundar. "Come on, Mykail, you sure sound like a girl sometimes. Doesn't he, brother?" Thundar nodded his head up and down saying yes because he could now understand every word in their native tongue. He just couldn't speak.

"Haha," laughed Mykail, a little embarrassed. "You know, it's bright, real royal," said Mykail.

"Oh okay then," replied Saka.

"It's just amazing, that's all. It's the opposite of where I live," said Mykail.

"And where exactly is that?" asked King O'Saka, closing the door from his study and now walking towards them.

"Good morning, Father," said Saka.

"Good morning, boys," replied the King.

"I live in …" Mykail started to say but was interrupted by the King.

"Hold on, before you start our friendship off with a lie, you and I both know you do not live in Bontiwo. Where do you live, son?" asked the King in a stern voice. Mykail stood quiet for a few seconds then said, " I'm homeless. Sorry I lied to you, Saka. I was afraid you would laugh at me. But I know now that you are not that type of person. You are not that type of people."

"You're homeless?" asked the Prince. " Where do you go every night, and where do you sleep? Where are your parents?" demanded the Prince.

"I don't know my real parents," replied Mykail. "The people who raised me said they found me deep in the forest where they lived. They were killed by a stampede of buffalo while hunting for food about three years ago. I've been living here and there ever since."

"Man, Mykail, you should have told me," said Prince Saka with disappointment in his eyes, almost in tears.

"Mykail, I'm sorry for your pain. Well you are with friends now, and I know Saka has an excellent day planned for you guys. So I'll let you get to it," said the King.

The next morning, sunlight beamed through the dark blue curtains of Saka and Thundar's window right into Saka's eyes. He awoke to find Mykail staring at him and Thundar nowhere to be found. He asked, "Where is Thundar?"

"Don't know," replied Mykail. Saka turned his head and laid in his bed a little longer. Thirty minutes later, there was a knock at the door. The door opened and a servant brought in enough breakfast to feed ten people. The Prince got up. Both of them ate. Saka got dressed, and they went looking for Thundar. They walked up and down the halls of the palace but did not see him until they decided to go outside. When they opened the doors to exit the palace, Thundar was sitting on the steps with his hand on his head as if he was in deep thought or worried about something.

"Morning, brother, are you okay?" asked Saka.

Thundar nodded his head yes, looking at Saka with a strange and tired look in his eyes.

"What's wrong, brother?" asked Saka, putting his hand on Thundar's shoulder.

Thundar began to sign. "Last night, I had the strangest dream. The contents of the dream are not what made it strange. It felt so real and, when I woke up this morning, my muscles felt like I had been running all night long."

"What was the dream about?" asked Saka.

"I remember I was swimming in what had to be the Victoria River because that's the single place I have ever swum. Then all of a sudden, I was running through the forest as if it was my first time. I remember falling and hurting my leg. After that, I put some sort of medicine on my wound. I made the medicine from plants and roots. I don't know how to do that. Brother, this was a most vivid dream."

"Are you okay now?" asked Mykail.

Thundar shook his head yes, and they went on into the forest.

Mykail spent many nights at the palace, sometimes staying for weeks at a time. The Prince grew taller and more handsome every day. He was in perfect physical condition with big, bright, light brown eyes and pearly white teeth. He excelled in all of his training, and all of the women in the kingdom admired him, young and old. Even though it seemed the potential for affection from women towards Saka was infinite, he never let it affect his studies and friendships. There was undoubtedly only one young woman to which he paid any genuine attention.

Zulin was the daughter of Master Yasufe. She was also his student, so she and Saka trained together most of the time. Zulin was two years older than Saka, smart and exotically beautiful. Sometimes she would sneak and go to the woods for a little while with the Prince, Thundar and Mykail because her father was very strict and did not approve of ample time spent playing.

Many years ago, Master Yasufe Hang, his wife and infant Zulin were exiled from Echizen province in Japan after a war his country lost. He was a great general, so they did not want to kill him. On the long voyage to the coast of Africa, his wife succumbed to chickenpox since they were not prepared to sail across the world and had not brought that specific medicine. He and his baby girl, Zulin, were shipwrecked on the African coast and brought to the King. His wife had died on the treacherous voyage to Africa.

King O'Saka knew of his great many battles and victories and was honored to meet him. He asked him to stay and become ageneral in his honor. He stayed and taught them how to forge swords and how to use them. Master Yasufe also introduced them to the martial arts and implemented a form of The Art of War into the army's strategical core. King O'Saka has the utmost respect for him, and all crucial decisions were made in consult with Master Yasufe and General Nakatu.

When Saka, Thundar and Mykail were twelve years old, Zulin was fourteen. They were all very mature for their age. The Prince and Zulin were little by little becoming more than friends, spending more and more time alone with each other. By now, both were experiencing the feelings and emotions of children their ages, and being around each other every day, training and playing together, made it hard to remain just friends.

Chapter VIII

Emerging Strengths

One beautiful sunny late afternoon, all four of them, exhausted from training, decided to call it a night. Saka told Thundar and Mykail to go ahead and he and Zulin would catch up with them later. So Thundar and Mykail went on their way.

They were almost home when Mykail said to Thundar, "I'm not ready to go in just yet. I want to continue walking for a while."

Thundar nodded his head and walked on towards the palace. Mykail turned around and started walking in the direction of the Prince and Zulin. Thundar noticed and was curious, so he doubled back and followed Mykail using the trees and staying high above him. When Mykail stopped walking, he knelt down behind some bushes about fifteen feet away from Saka and Zulin. Thundar perched himself in a tree to the right of her and watched as Mykail spied on their peers.

The Prince was holding Zulin very close and staring into her eyes. "I've never felt this way before, Saka. I'm scared," said Zulin, looking slightly away for a second.

"Why are you scared? There is no one who can compare to you. I would never do anything to hurt you. My first thought and my last before I fall asleep is of you," replied Saka.

"Oh, Saka, you are so sweet. If Thundar and Mykail knew how we honestly felt about each other, they'd probably be a little jealous," said Zulin.

"You think so?" asked the Prince.

"Well Thundar is so smart and so into his training that he probably wouldn't be, but Mykail is already acting a little strange," replied Zulin.

"What do you mean?" asked Saka.

"Sometimes he stares at us when we sit alone and talk. I see him staring at us as long as no one says anything. I can look at him to let him know that I see him, but he continues to stare right through me," said Zulin.

"He most likely has a crush on you. All the guys do. I'm just the lucky one out of many," said the Prince, pulling her a little closer so their noses touched.

Pushing the Prince softly, Zulin said, "I'm serious, Saka. He is a little peculiar. He hasn't grown any taller or changed bodywise in years."

"Huh," chuckled the Prince. "I've noticed. I guess his parents were small people, and he has done all the growing he is going to do. I don't know."

Meanwhile in the bushes, Mykail listened to every word with clinched fist, unaware that Thundar was watching close above.

"Now enough about Mykail," said the Prince as he kissed Zulin on the cheek.

"Saka, we have to go. It's getting late," she said. "Okay, but before I let you go …" said the Prince. Then they capped off the evening with a long, passionate kiss that for some reason enraged Mykail to tears.

Thundar patiently watched him as he ran off deep into the woods, crying. Thundar took his eyes off him briefly to get his footing and follow him but, just like that, he was gone. He even tried to pick up his scent, but there was none.

The next morning, Saka and Thundar met up after their lessons at the palace gates. Thundar hadn't told Saka what had happened yet. Now was as good a time as any. Saka was surprised and concerned about the situation. He asked Thundar not to do anything and told him that he would deal he never came. Eventually, Zulin showed up. "Hi, Prince. Hi, Thundar," she said.

"Hi, Zulin," replied Saka, while Thundar nodded his head hello. "Guys, I have a wonderful idea. My father is leaving as we speak for Borelsand to meet with the other generals. He will not be back for days. I was thinking we could go to the beach on Victoria Lake. I have never been. What do you think?" Zulin asked excitedly.

"My Father is going also," said Saka. "We'll need food and supplies. It is a full day's journey there and back. I'm with it. "I don't know. There are many dangers. We should not go," Thundar signed.

"Come on, Thundar. We will be careful and, besides, we have you as our guide. We leave early tomorrow in the morning," replied Saka.

"Yes!" screamed Zulin, as she grabbed the Prince and kissed him. Thundar just stood there and shook his head in disappointment.

Later that night, Saka and Thundar were conversing through sign while enjoying the beautiful view of the wonderful, deadly Treazur Lake. "Brother, this journey we are taking tomorrow is irresponsible and not like you. You are letting your feelings for Zulin cloud your otherwise sound judgment," said Thundar.

"Come on, not you too," said Saka, slightly upset. " Why have my two best friends suddenly become thorns in my side? We go deeper in the forest every day. This will merely change in depth a bit. It has nothing to do with Zulin. Father's gone, and we are due for a real adventure, wouldn't you say," said the Prince.

"Okay, Saka, I guess you're right," Thundar signed reluctantly.

The next morning, they met up at the spot, all suited up as if they were going to war and each carrying their weapon of choice: Saka his sword, Thundar his spear, and Zulin her sword.

"Well, off we go," said Saka as they went through the gates.

"Hey, wait for me," said a familiar voice from a distance.

"I knew you would make it," said Saka with a big smile. "We are going south to Victoria Beach."

"Really," said Mykail with a voice of concern. "That is a treacherous journey. Whose idea was that?

"Mine," answered Zulin. "Figures," murmured Mykail.

"Hey, we're leaving. Are you coming or not?" asked Saka.

"Yeah, I'm coming, but Zulin is supposed to be the oldest one of us, not the stupidest," said Mykail.

"What did you say?" screamed Zulin as she lunged at Mykail.

Thundar grabbed her and Saka shouted, "Stop this crazy mess right now!" They calmed down. "Now apologize to each other and shake hands. What is the problem? Especially you, Mykail, what is going on, man? What kind of gentleman talks to a lady like that?" said Saka.

"I'm sorry," said Mykail.

"Me too," replied Zulin.

"Well, can we go now?" asked the Prince, and they started on their way.

For hours and hours, they walked, joking and laughing while Thundar led the way. The amulet brought him through these parts before -- through Victoria Lake several times, but he always turned around after he got across. He didn't tell Saka, but he was pretty confident that he could navigate them there and back safely. He was the same age as Saka but, in primate years, he was a young adult already, and the use of the amulet had increased his maturity, knowledge and skills considerably.

"Have any of you been to Victoria Lake before?" asked Mykail.

"Yeah, I've been with my Father a couple of times."

"What about you, Mykail?" asked the Prince.

"Oh yeah, plenty of times! I used to live not too far from the beach. Where we are going is very beautiful. We still have a ways to go," replied Mykail.

Forty-five minutes went by. "I can smell the water from the lake now. Can you smell it, brother?" asked Saka.

Thundar took a big inhale and stopped in his tracks. Saka and the others also stopped walking and stared at Thundar.

"What's wrong, brother?" asked Saka.

"Hurry, Saka, take them and climb high in a tree," Thundar signed rapidly.

"Why, Thundar?" asked Saka.

"There are hyenas close by. Hurry," he signed.

"Let's go!" demanded Saka. They climbed high in a tall tree and waited. Thundar quickly climbed up in a tree close by and perched on a big branch with his spear in hand.

A few minutes passed and everything remained quiet until Mykail whispered to Saka, "I don't see anything." Suddenly, from the shadows two very large hyenas emerged, sniffing around in the bushes beneath them.

"Shhhh," said Saka, looking at Mykail and then at Zulin. When he turned his head to look back in Thundar's direction, he was terrified to see that Thundar had his spear in the air, pulled back and primed to throw it. Before he could say anything, Thundar threw the spear and jumped off the branch head- first diagonally towards the hyenas. The spear pierced the throat of one of the hyenas. Simultaneously, he switched positions in midair. Now his legs were first and slightly higher than his head. Then snap! He dropped a vicious flying elbow in the middle of the other hyena's back, hopped up and pulled his spear from the bloody neck of the now-dead carnivore and swiftly thrust it through the eye of the paralyzed predator. Saka, Zulin and Mykail were terrified, motionless. As Thundar pulled his spear from the deceased beast's eye socket, there was a rustle in the bushes behind him.

Saka yelled, "Thundar, behind you!"

Thundar turned around and cocked his spear back to throw but, before he could release it, another hyena sank its teeth into his throwing arm and yanked him down to the ground.

Saka screamed, "Noooo!" Then he leaped down with his sword raised high in the air, focused on the beast on Thundar's arm. But now he saw another wild carnivore has leaped to flank him. Thundar also saw the flanking K-9, so with his other hand he grabbed his spear, threw it toward the oncoming beast and punched the hyena on the arm. At the same time, Saka swung his sword down to the right, slashing the enormous K-9 in the face as Thundar's spear went all the way through its body. The swing and weight of Saka's blade caused him to spin, but he still kept his eyes on the animal attached to Thundar, remaining in control. And somehow when his feet hit the ground, the beast's body dropped to the dirt, leaving the severed head still attached to Thundar's arm.

"Brother, are you okay?" asked Saka, breathing heavily.

Thundar tried to pull the wild dog's head from his arm, but he could not, then he collapsed. Saka and the others grabbed him before he hit the ground.

After awhile, they pried the dead head from his arm, but he was bleeding very badly.

"Alright, brother, we have to go. Can you walk?" asked Saka.

Thundar nodded his head yes.

Wait," said Mykail, looking around for something. "We have to stop the bleeding and wrap his wound or he will not make it back."

"Okay!" replied Saka as he reached under his armor and tore off a piece of his shirt. "Use this," he said.

"Okay, one minute," said Mykail, grabbing a big purple leaf from the bushes. He knelt down, crushed the leaf in his hand and mixed it with some mud water. He then said some sort of prayer over it and rubbed it on the wound. Thundar immediately felt the effects of whatever Mykail had conjured up. They wrapped up his arm and headed homeward.

"We have to move fast. The scent of blood will attract more of those beasts and it getting dark," said Mykail.

"You're right," replied Saka as they moved swiftly through the rain forest with as much stealth as possible. Surprisingly, Thundar was walking without assistance and in a much better state than he was a little while ago. All of a sudden, Thundar stopped again, sniffing in the air.

"Are they here, brother?" asked Saka.

Thundar nodded his head yes and signed, "They are all around us! Hurry, into the trees."

"Not this time, brother, we do this together," said Saka, pulling out his sword. "Zulin and Mykail, into the trees now," he said. They did as he commanded and now Saka and Thundar were standing back to back. Now they could see that there were a lot more of the wild beasts and that they had circled them. One by one, they came out from behind the trees, snarling and snapping their teeth. Saka and his brother stood ready to fight for their lives, but there were too many hyenas and the chance ofsurvival was slim. As the beasts slowly closed in on them, Zulin sat high in a tree watching, frightened to death, but Mykail was standing on a branch with his arms stretched out to each side.

Zulin said,"Mykail, what are you doing? You're going to fall." Mykail's eyes were rolling to the back of his head and he was chanting something in another language, very low, over and over again.

It began to get very cold and started to lightning and thunder. Saka and Thundar had already killed at least five of them, but now they were falling without being struck. All of them one by one were dropping to the ground, howling in pain with froth coming out of their mouths.

Saka and Thundar could not understand what had just happened. They looked up in the trees at Mykail. He looked down at them, sluggishly closed his eyes and then fell down. Quickly, Thundar caught him before he hit the ground and, immediately, the weather went back to normal. Thundar laid him down and noticed that his arm did not hurt anymore and it was not bleeding, but there was blood coming from Mykail. He sniffed around until his nose ended up right between his legs. He stopped and looked up at the Prince with a startled, intense look on his face.

"What is it, brother?" asked Saka.

Thundar looked down at the area that was bleeding and abruptly tore the clothes from Mykail's groin. Neither of them could believe what they didn't see. They sat there for a minute or two just staring at each other. Zulin hopped down from the tree and yelled," Oh God, he's a girl!"

"What's going on?" said Saka, obviously confused.

As soon as he said that, Mykail opened her eyes, hopped up and ran off in the forest.

"Mykail!" screamed Saka, but she kept on running, surprisingly with no limp, and disappeared into the forest.

Saka, Thundar and Zulin spent the next ten minutes killing the miraculously wounded beast. Then they waited for Mykail, but she never came back, so they began the journey back home.

Chapter IX

Shetani (Home Sour Home)

In the other direction, Mykail ran franticly through the forest, crying. Her appearance gradually started to change from the young boy who never seemed to grow into a taller, beautiful teenage girl with heavenly brown eyes, high cheekbones and perfect skin the color of shaved mocha. She had jet-black, long, flowing locks with a single, red rose elegantly placed in them. Now instead of the old, torn clothes she wore as the young boy, she wore a breathtaking red dress that flowed down her body and rippled in the wind as she rapidly approached Victoria River. Out of the fog, a small, black rowboat presented itself perched on the bank. She got in it and began to row towards the other side of the river. The fog seemed to follow and cloak her perfectly until she could not be seen.

When she got to the other side and got off the boat, the fog followed her as she moved swiftly through the forest with more of a glide than a walk. She soon approached a large tree that was very old and wretched with not one leaf on its withered black branches. It had markings carved into it that circled around the bark of the tree. When she got about ten feet away from this wicked, evil-looking tree, the ground began to vibrate under her feet. She proceeded on and passed right through it as if it was water.

This was no ordinary tree. It obviously was some sort of magical portal to a place not seen by the naked eye. Now instead of endless forest, an enormous, black castle seemed to reach to the clouds. Black smoke pulsated from the top of it as if there were back-to-back explosions, but it was so quiet. All that could be heard was the strange sound of the wind mixed with the hissing of snakes, the chirping of crickets and the sound of lots of people moaning. It was a very disturbing mixture of sounds. Now in the distance by the castle doors, men in black and red armor stood guard, holding large chains with gigantic hyenas attached to the ends of the chains. They were the same kind of beasts that she, Saka and the others had encountered earlier. As she got closer, the hyenas started howling and barking. Then she raised her hands to the sky and, in the blink of an eye, she was inside the castle, lying across a huge bed draped in red linen.

The whole room was the color of fresh blood. Even the books on her bookshelf were in red and black covers. At first she just laid there for a while, staring at the very high and morbidly decorated ceiling lit with the flickering of candlelight. Then she began to weep for hours until she cried herself to sleep.

That night while she was fast asleep, a very tall and dark figure appeared by her bedside and just stood over her and watched as she slept. "My daughter … Icya, my beautiful daughter. What have you been into?" the very tall and dark figure whispered in a deep, hoarse, horrible voice.

"Get away from me. You are not my father," said the girl as she woke from her slumber.

"Then who am I, my sweet flower?" he asked.

"I don't know. You tell me. You look like Congion, you even sound like him, but my father would not have me out rambling through the forest at all hours of the night spying on people who do not even care what you are doing. Ever since I brought you that tormented book of evil spells from Treazur Lake, you have been a different person entirely," replied the young lady, scowling up at him.

"You have done a superb job, my lovely. I don't expect that I'll need you to spy on them anymore," Congion said with a grimacing grin.

"Father, what are you doing down there, all night and all day? You know what? Don't worry about it. Just go!" she screamed.

"As you wish, my dear," he said as he left the room at a snail's pace. She rested there a little while just staring at the ceiling then went to sleep.

The next morning, she woke up to three loud and peculiar females. "Ah look who at last decided to bless us with her presence," said Mama Yewande. The mother of the two identical twin sisters, Apunda and Yejide, was a big-boned, tall, well-shaped, dark-skinned woman who wore her hair in three very large puffs. Her daughters were pretty much miniatures of her, except they wore two puffs. The three were servants of the house of Congion in the faraway land of Shetani, and the mother was by all rights a voodoo priestess. The twins were Congion's daughters, just like Icya, but he treated Apunda and Yejide very poorly. Congion mentally and physically abused the twins and their mother often.

Congion's deceased wife, Solange, Icya's mother, died of an unknown disease and, over the years, rumors started going around that Mama Yewande had poisoned her so she could have Congion for herself. Congion, his wife and Mama Yewande all lived inside the palace in Ardhi Anasa before Saka's birth. Icya, Apunda and Yejide were all born in the palace. Mama Yewande was his best student and then became his apprentice.

Momma Yewande

Queen Nidera, Mama Yewande and Solange were thought to be best friends, but no one knew that Mama Yewande was Congion's mistress. She had gotten pregnant by him around the time the disease really took its toll on his wife. Solange died a year after Icya was born. The twins were born six months after that. King O'Saka caught Congion and Mama Yewande together on several occasions. He warned Congion that nothing good would come out of his infidelity, but Congion asked him to stay out of his business and continued in his adulterous ways. Congion was always a dark and dismal person but, after his wife died, he became even more so. He always gave Icya the best of everything and, when the twins were born, he truly loved them and he showed them love. But after the rumors spread, he disconnected himself from them, and the love soon turned to hate. He also kept Icya away from them.

After they got older, he even made them serve her, to both Icya's and the twins' dislike. Now he often used them for rituals too dangerous to perform on one person or for rituals that called for the possession of a human body. They had been possessed by strange and evil spirits so many times that a mere fraction of their human soul remained intact. They were jealous of Icya because she was the sole person in the world that Congion showed any kind of compassion. He truly loved her.

"What is it? What do you want?" asked Icya, a little irritated.

"Your bath is ready," said Mama Yewande.

"What? Have I died and gone to heaven? Oh and it's my birthday also? A bath, really," said Icya.

"Well, of course, we didn't prepare it for you," said Yejide.

"Look, you are bleeding all over your bed," said Apunda. Icya hopped up and went to the bath that had been prepared.

"What happened to you last night?" asked Apunda.

"Do you need some help in there?" asked Yejide, joking but not really.

"Don't play with me right now. I'm not in the mood," replied Icya.

"What have you been doing all these nights?" inquired Mama Yewande.

"I think she must have found her a man to lay with," said Apunda.

"A man, oh is that why you come home bleeding like a stuck pig," said Yejide. Both were breathing heavily, trying desperately to keep the demons inside them at bay.

"The both of you are in no place to speak of men and lying with them. Aye," she chuckled. "We all know why neither of you are frequently seen in the light of day, don't we? I don't believe I'll ever be into sharing men, or should I say sharing ugly, hairy, one-eyed, murderous demon monsters," said Icya, smirking intensely. The twins just stood there grinding and sucking on their teeth but not saying a word.

"What are you going on about child?" asked Mama Yewande.

"They know exactly what I'm talking about. And, oh yeah, he really stinks. Both of you smell just like him. You can't even wash it off, can you?" said Icya, getting out of the tub and wrapping a towel around herself.

"What is she talking about?" demanded Mama Yewande. "I don't know," the twins said nervously at the same time.

"Well, do you know Cotto or, better yet, the Popobawa, man by day, demon by night?" said Icya.

"Shut up, you stupid idiot," screamed Apunda.

"I'll kill you," screamed Yejide, lunging at Icya but held back by Mama Yewande.

"Is this true? No, it is true. Isn't it?" demanded Mama Yewande, pulling Apunda by the hair and slapping Yejide down to the ground at the same time.

"No, Mama!" screamed Apunda. "Let's go," she yelled, as she dragged both of them out of the room by their hair.

Chapter X

Who's That Girl

Eight months later, Icya decided that it had been long enough since she'd seen Prince Saka and to no coincidence that day was Saka's birthday.

"Nettie (one of the female servants), come here, Nettie," called Icya.

"Yes, Princess, what do you need?" replied Nettie. "I'm hungry. Bring me something to eat!" she demanded. Nettie brought Icya some fruit, meat, bread and butter on a tray. Icya ate and offered Nettie some of the food. Nettie graciously declined and then asked Icya, "So what are you going to do today?"

"Well, I'm glad you asked because I'm going somewhere and I want you to go with me," replied Icya.

"Really!" said Nettie, with much excitement in her voice.

"Yes, really," said Icya

"Where are we going?" she asked.

"Don't worry your big head. Are you not happy to be getting out of this dark, boring, decrepit, haunted old castle? I mean if you don't want to go, just let me know," said Icya, cleaning her mouth with a cloth as she finished the food that Nettie had prepared for her.

"No, no, no, please I want to go," said Nettie, grabbing the tray from Icya's bed.

"Well, go put that up and hurry back," said Icya. Nettie hurried back.

"Okay, I'm ready," said Nettie.

"Oh no you're not! You're not going anywhere with me dressed like that," said Icya, laughing a little. Nettie had on a green and white dress with ruffles at the bottom that covered her from her esophagus to her ankles. "We're gonna show a little skin today. Don't worry, I have something for you to wear," said Icya with a sneaky smile on her face. Then she went to her closet and pulled out two beautiful dresses for them to wear.

Both were red and black, skin-tight and stopped right above their knees. They got dressed, and Nettie was somewhat skeptical about the cleavage that the dress revealed.

"Uhhh, Princess, I don't know about this. You sure this is safe to be wearing in front of people? And look at yours, it's worse than mine," said Nettie, trying to stuff some of her ample bosom down into the dress.

"Shut up. Everything will be fine. Let's go," replied Icya as she dabbed perfume on her neck and groin area.

"My Princess, are you planning to give some lucky fellow some of the royal goodies?" Nettie asked jokingly.

"Hush now, I just like being fresh. It's hot out there," replied Icya.

"How are we supposed to get to wherever we are going?" asked Nettie.

"Be quiet and hold on to me." Icya pulled Nettie onto the bed and then started chanting an ancient tongue. In a split second, both of them were standing outside in the forest by that wicked-looking tree. "What's going on, where are we and what is wrong with that tree? I'm not going in there," said Nettie.

"Yes, you are. Come on," yelled Icya as she yanked Nettie by the arm pulling her inside the wretched tree. They passed through the tree, walked a little ways, then got on the mysterious boat that Icya had traveled on before. After they crossed the river, Icya brought them to another large tree; they passed through it and came out of another similar tree right behind the Ardhi Anasa palace gates close to Treazur Lake.

"Oh my God! What is this?" asked Nettie.

"We are in Ardhi Anasa, home of the Great Moor King O'Saka Navitazi," replied Icya.

"What are we doing here?" asked Nettie.

"Aye, be quiet before they hear us," replied Icya. "Before who hears us?" whispered Nettie, looking around to see who Icya was talking about

"Them," whispered Icya as she pointed toward Zolatar and Volaris running around like usual.

"Aye … what is that? Oh my goodness, we have to get out of here," said Nettie, attempting to turn around and run.

"Shhhhh! Come on, let's go before they see us," said Icya as she grabbed Nettie's hand and quietly crept around to the front of the palace.

The courtyard of the palace overflowed with people from everywhere, all different colors and creeds and, in the center of it all, there was a long line of people with gifts.

"Who are the gifts for?" asked Nettie.

"They are for Prince Saka, the son of King O'Saka. It is his birthday," replied Icya.

"Do you both know each other?" asked Nettie.

"Yeah we kinda … well, it's complicated," replied Icya, looking downward.

"Aye, I didn't bring him anything. Damn, what am I gonna do," said Icya, shaking her leg like she had to pee.

"Stay right here. I have to go pee," she said as she ran off to some nearby bushes to urinate.

As soon as she left, Nettie spotted a very nicely dressed guy sitting on a bench with a beautifully decorated box on the ground beside him. Nettie walked nonchalantly and got behind the man, bent down on her hands and knees and slid the box under the bench. "Yes," she said as she ran back to the spot where she and Icya were.

"Where were you and what is that?" asked Icya, smiling a little.

"I got this for you. A gift for letting me come along," she replied.

"Okay then," said Icya as they ran nearly to the front of the line.

"Excuse me, may we cut in please?" asked Nettie as they cut in the line in front of a young man about their age. The young man was so taken by Icya's beauty that he didn't even notice Nettie or that they had just cut in line. Now they could see Saka.

"Oh my! So that's the Prince? I see why you came all the way through the forest to get here. He is so fine," said Nettie, sucking on her teeth while looking the Prince up and down.

"He's okay," replied Icya, smiling to the side.

"Oh no! Look at our shoes! They are filthy from the walk here," said Nettie.

"Here, dust mine off," said Icya as she took hers off and handed them to Nettie. Nettie patted them together and got off as much dust as possible. "Well, I guess that will have to do," said Icya as she put her shoes back on, drawing a lot of attention to herself.

Saka stood there in his royal clothing, wearing a white head wrap and holding the sword that his father had given him. He had it tucked in an elegant, wide golden belt. In the short time since Icya had seen him last, he had gotten bigger and taller.

King O'Saka and Thundar were there, dressed in the same manner, and the five elders were standing behind them. Now, one person stood between them and Icya's secret love.

The person in front of them presented Prince Saka with a gift, but before Saka could thank him and shake his hand, his eyes locked with Icya and they gazed at each other for a while until Zulin walked up and stood between them. The guy who was giving his present to Saka was so busy looking at the two ladies that he forgot that the Prince didn't shake his hand.

"Happy birthday, my handsome Prince," said Zulin as she handed him a small colorfully wrapped box and kissed him on the cheeks.

Then as she looked back at Icya with the evil eye, Nettie walked up to them and said," Happy birthday, Prince Saka. Here is a gift from Princess Icya of

Shetani. Icya moved to the side, and Nettie held out her hand so that Icya could grab it and come greet the Prince.

"How do you do, Princess Icya of Shetani? So gracious of you to come this far for this celebration," said the Prince as he grabbed her hand and respectfully kissed the top of it.

"Happy birthday, Prince Saka, and to you, Thundar, I also wish the same," said Icya. Thundar nodded his head to thank her. By now, the majority of the men who were in line were standing on the side of the line trying to get a good look at the three women standing near Prince Saka.

"It's kind of you to say happy birthday to Thundar. So you are from Shetani? That must have been a long journey," said the Prince.

"Yes, it was, but I would have traveled across the world to meet the great Prince Saka and his famous companion, Thundar," she replied.

"Well, thank you for coming. Zulin, this is Princess Icya from the kingdom of Shetani," said Saka, looking to the side at Zulin as she watched them with a hawk's eye.

"I heard. It is a pleasure," said Zulin, gritting her teeth. "And to you the same," replied Icya, sucking her teeth. "Okay then," said Prince Saka.

"Well if you need anything, just let us know," said King O'Saka.

"Hopefully we will see each other again before I leave," said Icya as they turned around and walked away. Prince Saka continued to meet and greet his guests.

"Oh Princess, that was intense," said Nettie.

"No, that was the best. That went perfectly. Come on, time to go home now," said Icya.

"Already?" replied Nettie with a disappointed look on her face.

"Yep, let's go! Mission accomplished," said Icya as they started on their way home.

After they got back to Shetani, they laid down for a while on Icya's bed, talking and laughing. Caught up in the moment, Icya reminisced and shared with Nettie some stories of the adventures she had with Saka and the others in the form of Mykail (her little brother who had died of unknown causes a year before she met Saka).

Mykail was born in the Shetani palace. He was treated the same as the twins, but Icya and Mykail were the best of friends, and she took up for him all the time. He and his other siblings were like oil and water. They never got along and were constantly at each other's throats. His death devastated Icya and Mama Yewande. During his period of sickness, Icya and Mama Yewande pulled together to try to save him, but all of their efforts failed.

Icya and Nettie continued talking, and Icya finally told Nettie how she truly felt about Prince Saka and that even though she and Zulin did not get along all the time, she still thought of her as a friend. Nettie asked her if she would ever reveal to Saka and the others that she was Mykail, who Mykail actually was, and who her father is. Icya said she would have to one day if she wanted to regain Saka's trust. They continued to converse until they went to sleep.

Chapter XI

Hush

In the middle of the night, Nettie woke up and decided to go to her room. She got up, tucked Icya under the covers, quietly tiptoed out of the room and shut the door behind her. As she walked down the hall towards her room, she heard someone talking and, before she could see who it was, someone said,

"Aye, Nettie, where are you going with all that jelly?" It was the twins. Nettie just kept walking, trying desperately to make it to her room before they caught up with her. "Aye, this one must have a hearing problem," said Apunda to her sister.

"Come here, Nettie," yelled Yejide as she raised her hand slightly and chanted two or three words. Nettie's body tensed up, then she stopped, turned around and began to walk towards the twisted twins.

"That's more like it. Where have you been, Nettie? What have you been doing all day with Icya?" asked Apunda.

"Nothing, we just took a walk to town and took a little stroll through the forest for a little while, that's all," replied Nettie with a straight face.

"Why are you lying to us, Nettie?" asked Yejide. "I thought we were friends," said Apunda.

"I'm not lying. Why would I do that and we are friends," replied Nettie, swallowing nervously.

"Okay friend, let's take a walk. Sister, wouldn't you like to go for a walk? It's a nice night tonight," said Yejide as she grabbed Nettie by the hand.

"I would love to go for a walk, sis," replied Apunda as she grabbed Nettie's other hand and forced her to go with them.

"I'm tired. I, I just want to go get something to eat and go to sleep," said Nettie, looking back and forth at each twin.

"Don't worry, it will be a short walk," said Yejide. They walked all the way to the end of the long, dark hall and then threw Nettie on the ground.

"So, Miss Princess is in love with Prince Saka, huh, and today was his birthday. I cannot wait to tell mother that little precious piece of information. We were listening to your whole conversation, you little liar," said Apunda as both of them pinned Nettie down and slapped her several times in her face.

"Please stop," begged Nettie. "Okay, we'll stop. Just tell us how you got to Ardhi Anasa," said Yejide.

"I don't really know how. Icyaaaaa," yelled Nettie, but she could not be heard from this far.

"Shut up!" screamed Apunda as she raised her hand in front of Nettie's face and chanted a few words. In a split second, Nettie's mouth and nostrils sealed up completely. She could not breathe. They let her up and she tried to run, but Apunda tripped her and she fell down again. Yejide then pinned her down and looked her square in the eyes for about a minute, just watching her as she suffocated. Nettie's eyes were bucked and full of tears as she kicked and tried to scream. "Okay Nettie, do you want to talk now?" asked Apunda in a calm voice. Nettie shook her head yes. Apunda mushed Nettie in the face, and Nettie's mouth and nostril holes reappeared.

"Talk!" screamed Yejide as Nettie laid there gasping for air. After she caught her breath, she told them everything. They harassed her for a while, then they let her go and went on about their business. Nettie got up, went to her room and cried all night until she went to sleep.

Chapter XII

This Is Only a Test

For the months that followed, Nettie kept quiet about what had happened with the twins and everything was as normal as could be expected. Icya stayed to herself and kept her head buried in books, becoming more and more enlightened in the world of voodoo and black magic. Her powers grew, and so did her feelings for Saka! As much as she tried to put them in the past, she could not shake the deep affection that she felt for him and the true friendship that she had forged with the others. Every few weeks, she would transform into a bird and visit Ardhi Anasa to maybe get a glimpse of Saka and, even though she could, she would never go inside the palace. Sometimes she would see them and just watch, but other times she would not see them at all.

Saka and Thundar did not play together as much as they used to, but when she did see them running through the forest, it put a big smile on her face. Seeing Saka and Zulin together was not always a happy occasion for Icya. While the feelings she had for Saka were one-sided, Saka and Zulin's love for each other grew mutually stronger by each passing day, and it was easy to see.

A year had gone by since Saka's birthday celebration. Icya had dresses made for her and Nettie especially for the occasion. In less than three days, she would get to see him and maybe talk to him, if not just for a brief moment. This thought alone brought a smile to her face that would light up a pitch- black cathedral. Both Icya and Nettie were excited about going to the celebration. They had been speaking about it for weeks. This time they would be prepared with gifts so they would not have to steal one from someone. Icya had also planned to use her father's old carriage so they would arrive in a grand fashion and their shoes would not be scuffed up like last time.

About a week back, one afternoon right before dark, after reading a few pages of one of her many books, Icya decided to make a quick visit to Ardhi Anasa and see if they were setting up for the celebration, just to make sure it was still ago. Feeling a little happier than usual, and a little anxious, she chose to walk out of the palace door and then through the gates. Any other time, she would have used the hidden portal she had conjured up under her bed to get outside the gates.

It was getting late, so she left her room and closed the door behind her. From down the hall, she heard, "Where are you going at this late hour, my dear?" It was Mama Yewande.

"For a walk," replied Icya as she continued down the hall and out the castle door. As soon as she got outside, she put a black scarf over her head and walked swiftly because she noticed the guards were looking up towards the top of the castle for some reason. She stopped, turned around and looked in the direction they were looking but did not see anything so she kept going. It took her about twenty minutes to get to the front gate.

After she got outside the gate, she turned and looked again into the night sky but did not see anything unusual so she continued on to the tree portal. When she finally got to the wretched looking tree, the birds in the treetops were suddenly disturbed. She stopped and abruptly turned all the way around, but she still could not see anything because it was so dark.

For a while, the animals and the birds were in an uproar, but, after a few minutes, everything got quiet. Frightened a little, Icya waited and surveyed the area but, in this darkness, she could not see anything so she went ahead through the portal. When she got to the other side, she went and hid behind a tree to see if anyone had followed her, but no one exited the portal. After a few minutes, she began to walk towards the next portal and before she could walk ten good steps, it happened again. The wildlife around her became highly disturbed. She instantly transformed into a peregrine falcon and swiftly flew to and through the portal. Certain that nothing could have followed her from that point, she continued and saw what she had journeyed to see. Indeed, the kingdom of Ardhi Anasa was gearing up for the big celebration. This made her very happy. On the way home, she sliced through the air and trees, passing through the portal with precise speed and agility so that it would be impossible for anyone to follow her.

Late that night, right before sunrise, Popobawa went to Congion's room after he summoned him. When he got to the door of the room, bending over and squeezing his wings together trying to fit inside the doorway, he could hear the faint sound of chanting, but he could not see where it was coming from. A human could not have heard this. He looked to Congion's bed and saw him in a deep sleep, lying on his back shirtless, with his arms crossed like a dead person in a casket. One of his female servants was sleeping with her head on his stomach, so the chanting wasn't coming from him. He then called out to Congion but got no response, so he walked closer to the bed. Popobawa now noticed that with each step he took closer to the bed, it got colder then extremely cold. By his third step, his right leg from his calf muscle on down had frozen.

Screaming in pain, he hurriedly pulled his leg back and slammed into the wall, knocking a picture down behind him.

After his leg thawed out, he kept his distance and walked around to the other side of the bed. The chanting was louder now, and it was coming from a closet in the corner close to the head of the bed. He opened the closet and saw Mama Yewande surrounded by candles, sitting with her legs crossed amd rocking back and forth in a trance, chanting ancient words repeatedly. He then bent down, got face to face with her and screamed her name as loud as he could. His fowl spit splashed in her face, and her hair puff blew back as she broke from the trance, horrified at the sight, sound and smell of Popobawa.

Accomplishing what he had set out to do, he then turned around to the bed and walked towards it with no problem. Before he could call Congion's name, Congion opened his eyes and asked, "Is it done?"

"Yes," replied the monster, rolling his eyes with complete disgust on his face.

"What did you do, slave?" asked Congion.

"I spread the powder over the graves," he replied as he exhaled and looked down to the side.

"As evenly as possible over the entire gravesite?" asked Congion in a stern voice.

"Yes ahhhhr!" yelled Popobawa as he grabbed his chest in agony and left the room, bumping into the wall and hitting his head in the doorway. As a horrific transformation took place in the hallway, Congion woke the servant and told her to go get Nettie to help her wipe down his room to cleanse it of the monster's stench. Congion went back to sleep, and Mama Yewande again began chanting the protection spell.

Chapter XIII

Unexpected Guest

For Icya, time seemed to go by at a snail's pace, but now the day of the celebration was at hand. She was already up before dawn getting ready, and Nettie came as soon as she finished cleaning Congion's room.

"You look tired, Nettie," said Icya as she adjusted the hat that Nettie was wearing.

"Thank you, Princess," replied Nettie sarcastically. "You already know how beautiful you are. These dresses are the best," said Nettie as she ran both of her hands downward from her hips to her thighs, looking in the mirror. The dresses they wore were red and black with lace backing, and the bottom of the dresses, which stopped right above the knee, was lace. Icya had designed them herself, and they were sure to cause many heads to turn.

"Hand me that perfume over there," said Icya. Nettie handed her the perfume, and she proceeded to put some on her neck and ample around her groin area.

"Why do you put so much smell-good on, my Princess?" asked Nettie as she grabbed the bottle and put a little on her neck.

"It is hot out there. I don't want to get there and be smelling like a baby cheetah butt," said Icya, laughing heartily.

"Hahaha," chuckled Nettie, looking at the Princess with one eyebrow up.

"This time I got us a room in Mwana, a little village, a mile east of the Ardhi Anasaian palace. I have a few relatives there. Now we can go back the next day and have a little fun," said Icya with one of her eyebrows up. " Well, grab the gifts. Let's get out of here," said Icya, getting closer to her bed.

Nettie grabbed the two nicely decorated small boxes, put them in their suitcase, and got really close to Icya and said, "Oh no! I hate this part."

Icya put her arms around Nettie, said a few ancient words and in a split second they were outside the palace gates standing beside her father's carriage and horses. In a short time, they had passed through the first portal and into the kingdom of Ardhi Anasa. Before they entered the gates, they heard trumpets sounding off, pronouncing the beginning of the celebration. Inside the gates, there were games, magic shows, clowns, musicians, dancers, fighting tournaments and much more. It was by far the biggest celebration the kingdom had ever seen. There were so many people, there was barely room to walk and in the middle of everything was a huge stage.

"Oh, my God, This is amazing. Aye! The king must really love his boy. Huh! This is crazy. I have never seen anything like this in my life."

"Me either. There are so many people here. I hope we can get close enough to talk to him," said Icya as a guard stopped their carriage and let them know that they must proceed on foot from that point on. Icya and Nettie got down out of the carriage, and the guard gave them a ticket. The guard then unleashed the horses from the harness and took them to give them food and water.

"Okay, Nettie, let's have a little fun," said Icya as she took off her shoes and ran towards one of the gaming areas. For hours, they went from game to game and from event to event until it was time for the presentation of gifts to the Prince. This time, they made sure that they were not all the way in the back of the line.

"Saka and Thundar are going to love their gifts. I cannot wait to, Nettie, where are the gifts?" asked Icya.

"Oh no! They're in the suitcase in the carriage," replied Nettie.

"Aye! Hurry up and go get them," said Icya. "I'm going," replied Nettie as she ran to find the carriage. A half an hour had passed and Nettie had not come back with the presents, and Icya was almost at the front of the line.

"Where are you?" Icya whispered to herself. There were five more people in front of Icya when someone announced that King O'Saka was to present his gifts to both Saka and Thundar at this time and that the rest of the people who had presents for them could present theirs after him. At this very moment, Zulin was presenting Saka and Thundar with presents. She then kissed Saka and stood slightly behind him and Thundar. The line behind Icya was still very long, but the people got out of line to get a better view of the king's presentation.

Again, trumpets blew majestic chords as the speaker of the ceremony introduced the King of Ardhi Anasa, King O'Saka Navitazi.

The King walked to the podium in a cool and calm manner and said, "Good afternoon, people of Ardhi Anasa and traveling visitors from abroad. We thank you for taking the time out of your trying and busy lives to join us in celebrating the seventeenth birthdate of my two boys, Prince Saka and Prince Thundar. (Crowd cheers.) I am so proud of both of them. They have grown to be the best sons any man could hope for. They have even surpassed my expectations.

"Over the years they have received many gifts, some have been given twice so they have two of many things. So I'm sure you can guess the age-old question that has been marinating in my mind for over half a year. What do you give someone who has everything? Right! Well, about a month ago, I at last thought of the one present to put all others to shame. I'd give them something that is perfectly unique and there is only one to give. Well there are two, but anyway this gift should be always perceived as their passage into manhood. Now without further ado, I present to my sons, Prince Saka and Prince Thundar, my fourth and fifth most prized possessions, Zolatar and Volaris," shouted the King with his hands stretched out towards the palace.

Saka and Thundar looked at each other with big smiles on their faces and Saka said, "Okay then!" As soon as he said that, the ground started shaking and a large cloud of dust made its way towards the stage. Some of the people in the crowd were frightened. People were pulling out weapons that they were not supposed to have. Little kids were crying, and some of the people were running and hiding. By now, Icya had grabbed Nettie by the hand and they had made their way onto the stage. Meanwhile, Saka and the rest of the royals were on stage laughing uncontrollably. Now the big cloud of dust was right in front of the stage and everything got quiet. After the dust cleared, Zolatar and Volaris were kneeled down in front of the stage with their short arms stretched out in front of them and their noses touching the ground.

"Which one is mine, Father?" asked Saka with a huge smile on his face.

"Zolatar is yours, my son," replied the King. Then Prince Saka looked at Thundar and, in a split second, both of them jumped in the air and landed on the raised saddles that set atop the Terroraptors. They grabbed the reins and pulled on them tightly. Then Zolatar and Volaris howled loudly, stood up straight and jumped fifteen feet in the air, then came down with a thunderous boom.

Back on stage, despite the delay, Nettie made it with the gifts. She handed them to Icya.

Icya yelled, "Hey, Prince Saka, Thundar, catch," as she threw the gifts to them. They caught the gifts and then opened them in front of everyone. Two beautiful gold bracelets spiraled up from the wrist to the elbow. They both put them on and raised the bracelets in the air. Everyone thought the gifts were great and applauded except Zulin. She scowled and gritted her teeth at Icya while Icya and everyone else watched and marveled at the two Princes as they gracefully pranced around on top of the grand master rhinos.

About two hours had passed and it was starting to get dark. Saka and Thundar had just gotten off Zolatar and Volaris and were now accepting gifts again. Zulin was standing beside Saka. Icya and Nettie were still on stage, now conversing with King O'Saka.

"So, Princess Icya, where exactly is Shetani?" asked the King.

"It's very, very far from here. Two hundred miles south of the Victoria River," replied Icya.

"So you travel all that distance, practically by yourself, to attend my boy's birthday celebration?" asked King O'Saka with a stern and intrigued look on his face.

"Well, not exactly. This entire trip is actually for my good friend Nettie," said Icya as Nettie stared at her with a slightly confused look on her face.

"Oh really! How so?" inquired the King.

"She truly believes that she's found her one true love and, unfortunately, a long and grueling trip here was the only way for her to see him and relieve me briefly from her terrible nighttime weeping and wailing," said Icya.

"So you have taken a liking to one of my fine guards?" asked King O'Saka.

"Nope, it's not a guard. It's the Prince," said Icya, smiling to the side.

"Well, I'm afraid Prince Saka is taken," replied the King.

"No, King O'Saka. Thundar is her man," said Icya, laughing aloud.

"Princess, please," said Nettie, slightly embarrassed but laughing a little.

"Hahaha! You're funny," said King O'Saka as he laughed heartily.

"All jokes aside, tell me. Why do you travel so far?" asked King O'Saka.

"Well, King O'Saka, I really don't leave the kingdom much and your land is very beautiful, one might even say exotic to my countrymen. So when I do get a chance to get away, I make it worth the trip. I mean, look around, this is like a dream, and where I'm from, Saka and Thundar the Gorilla Prince are a constant topic of children and young adults' conversation," she replied.

"Okay then! You know, Shetani is one of the very few places of which I know little about. Is King Ade still ruler?" asked the King but, before Icya could answer, General Nakatu walked up to King O'Saka and whispered something in his ear.

"Really? Bring it here!" said King O'Saka to General Nakatu.

"As you wish," replied General Nakatu as he walked off the stage.

"I'm sorry, Princess, but I have to attend to a pressing matter. We will continue this conversation later," said the King as he walked over to Saka, grabbed him by the shoulders and whispered something in his ear.

Meanwhile, on the other side of the stage, Icya was asking Nettie why it had taken so long to bring back the gifts. She told Icya that the guards had moved the carriage from where it was at first and that they were acting weirdly.

"After I asked around and finally found the carriage, I had to sneak and get the suitcase out of it because they would not let anybody get near it," said Nettie.

"Aye! What's going on?" said Icya as she watched her carriage being brought near the stage.

King O'Saka walked off the stage and over to the carriage, circled it a couple of times, opened it up, looked inside and in a demanding voice said, "Who traveled here in this carriage?" No one gave him a reply. "Guards, retrieve all of the tickets from the visitors who benefited from carriage detail," commanded King O'Saka.

"Oh Yeshua! Someone must have recognized my father's old carriage and told him. Why did I come here in that old bucket anyway?" said Icya as she grabbed Nettie's hand.

"What's wrong, Princess?" asked Nettie a little concerned.

"We have to go now," whispered Icya as she pulled Nettie by the hand towards the back of the stage.

Meanwhile, the guards had not found the owner of the carriage, so King O'Saka told General Nakatu to find out which guard had taken the ticket for the carriage. General Nakatu found the guard near the front gate and brought him to King O'Saka. The King asked the guard if he remembered who owned that particular carriage. The guard thought about it for a minute or two, then he remembered and told the king that it belonged to two beautiful women dressed in red and black. King O'Saka thought about it for a little while, then one of his eyebrows went up and he turned his head around towards the spot Icya and Nettie were standing.

"Guards, look for two women dressed in red and black dresses," said King O'Saka.

Then the guard who gave them the ticket said, "Look, sire, there they are leaving from the back of the stage." King O'Saka spotted them but, as soon as he did, multiple people in the crowd start screaming in terror. The King turned his head slowly away from Icya and Nettie towards the screaming but, in the corner of his eyes, he saw a bird carrying a small animal. It flew away from the exact spot he had seen Icya and Nettie.

When his gaze firmly set on the screaming crowd, he could not believe what he saw: dozens of corpses raised from the grave walking amongst the living. Most of the corpses were the recently dead.

"Father, how can this be?" asked Saka as he pushed Zulin behind him and Thundar put himself between Saka and the uninvited guest.

"These walking dead are from the east cemetery. I recognize some of them. Someone has disturbed their rest. Nakatu, the arisen corpses do not seem to be attacking anyone. Get everyone inside. Sever the heads from the bodies, and send our dead back from where they came. Leave just one walking. Have a man follow it until it stops walking, then report the location!" commanded King O'Saka. The soldiers did as they were told and, within a few hours, all but one of the walking dead were immobilized and reburied.

ChapterXIV

Mice and a Rat

Later that night after everything had returned to as normal a state as possible, the King, General Nakatu, Master Yasufe and the five elders met up in the king's study.

"Someone who knew Saka's birthdate or, at least, knew that the celebration would take place today planned this. Was there anything of note from the investigation of the disturbed graves that could shed some light on who is responsible for this?" asked King O'Saka.

"We found a white powder spread over almost the whole cemetery and have concluded that Mwehu, a very dangerous and powerful mixture of voodoo and medicine used in summoning rituals, was brought upon our beloved dead. The dead are caused to rise and walk until they reach the place the ritual was performed. Only the recently dead skeletons were intact and strong enough to make it above ground," said Elder Sheshon (the oldest of the five elders and the kingdom's closest thing to a voodoo priest since Congion left).

"This is already known to me, Elder Sheshon. I was hoping that you and the majority of everyone here had come to the same conclusion as to who the culprit was, as I have," said King O'Saka, looking at each person in the room.

"Is Congion the person you speak of? Because if he is, I am not sure I agree. We have not seen or heard a peep from him for many, many years now. Why would he come back just to crash a party?" asked Elder Sheshon.

"The words you speak, are they out of fear? Is the carriage that we confiscated the one Congion was last seen in? Is that Congion's carriage?" asked the King.

"Yes," replied Nakatu and Master Yasufe. The five elders were hesitant to answer.

"Answer me," said King O'Saka in a very stern voice. The other four elders nodded their heads yes. Eventually, Elder Sheshon did the same. "Okay then! The young woman claiming to be a Princess of Shetani came here in his carriage and by the look of her could be his daughter. She obviously had something to do with what happened tonight. When I think of it, Icya was his daughter's name. She was an infant when he vanished. She would be a teenager now," said the King.

"The men are out looking for her now," said General Nakatu.

"She might be a little hard to find. If my eyes were not playing tricks on me, I saw her shape-shift into a bird and her friend into a mouse. They flew off into the night," said King O'Saka, unaware that under the very seat that he sat in, Icya and Nettie were in the form of two white mice listening to everything the men said.

"So what do you want me to do? What kind of bird was it, sire?" asked General Nakatu.

"It was a peregrine falcon, possibly the fastest animal in the whole world. Well, by all means, keep looking for them. I was just making it plain that this was not one of those situations where you could say, 'Well, she could not have gone too far.' With that being said, we should be more careful. Put more men on guard. We have no idea what that was about or what Congion may be planning or has already started in motion. As of now, does anyone have anything to add? Okay then! Let's all get some sleep, and we will talk again tomorrow," said King O'Saka.

Before General Nakatu left the room, King O'Saka asked him to find Thundar and to tell him to come see him now.

Everyone except the King, Icya and Nettie left the room and went home or to the quarters. King O'Saka sat in his seat for a while with his hand on his chin deep in thought, then he hopped up, walked to his bookshelf, moved one book that moved five books at the same time, and pulled a small chest from the hidden area. He grabbed a medallion out of the box and put it on and, soon after, Thundar knocked on the door of the study.

"Come in, my son. Go and put your amulet on. I would like to have an enlightened thought session, if you don't mind," said the King. Thundar grabbed the amulet and put it on. Again, the power of the amulet brought them to their knees, causing a blinding light to pour from their eyes. The wind circled them, coming from all corners and strumming perfect chords on the long-neck lute that always sat in the same spot. The twisting wind was strong enough to blow Icya and Nettie out in the open from under the chair. Luckily, neither King O'Saka nor Thundar saw them before they could scurry into a dark corner.

After everything subsided, the king and son sat down. They talked and brainstormed for two hours. Shortly after, Thundar took off the medallion, put it up, said goodnight and went to his room. King O'Saka sat a little while longer in thought, then got up, walked to a large couch, took off his shoes, laid down and went to sleep.

As soon as Icya was sure that he was asleep, she crawled up on the back of the couch, got as close to King O'Saka as possible without waking him and for a minute just stared at the medallion until King O'Saka adjusted himself and turned on his side. Then Icya hopped off the couch, and she and Nettie ran out of a small hole in the wall and started going out of the palace. As soon as they got outside, Icya changed into a bird, gently grabbed Nettie the mouse within her talons and flew off into the night sky.

Meanwhile, a soldier on horseback, assigned to apprehend the walking corpse, had followed it to the south portal and was now contemplating going through. He looked at the deformed, wretched tree, stuck his torch inside, and shook his head because the flame turned black while it was inside the portal. Then he loosened the reins on the horse and nudged the animal to go forward, but the horse refused, bucked him off and ran away, leaving the soldier behind. Now in pain from the fall, the guard got up, shook it off and stepped into the tree. When he got through, his torch took awhile to transition from the black flame to a regular flame, so he could not see the dead man walking.

As soon as the flame began to burn brightly again, he sprinted about fifty yards to try to catch the arisen corpse. Finally, he caught up with it and started marking trees so he could find his way back. He followed for almost an hour until it came upon the Victoria River. Then the upright cadaver walked into the river and was instantly carried under and downstream. The guard stayed around for thirty to forty-five minutes to see if it would wash up on the other side, but he could not see across the river in the dark, so he turned around and found his way back to the palace.

Chapter XV

Puppet on a String

Back in Shetani, Icya was infuriated and about to blow her top with but only one resource of ventilation, Nettie. "Oh that's just perfect. Now I can never go back as myself to Ardhi Anasa. What reason would Congion have for raising the dead and crashing Saka's party like that. It just doesn't make any sense at all," said Icya, pacing back and forth in her room.

"I'm sorry, Princess," said Nettie.

"Everything was so beautiful. It was perfect until they noticed his old, raggedy carriage. Why did I bring that old thing," Icya whispered to herself, now crying a little.

"Aww, it's okay, Princess Icya. I am sure you will think of something. You always do," said Nettie as she grabbed Icya and attempted to hug her.

"What Nettie! What can I do now? They think that I did that. They think that I am evil. I am not evil. I would never do something like that to Saka. I love him. He'll never love me now. What am I gonna do?" yelled Icya as she pushed Nettie off of her and sat on the bed crying a river.

"Look, I know you're in a dark place now, my friend, but you're smart. You are the smartest person I know. Just wait and see. You'll come up with another bright idea, sure as the sun will shine another day," said Nettie, standing beside Icya with her hand on her shoulders. As soon as she said that, Icya's eyes slowly started to come up from the ground. Now she was staring Nettie in her eyes with a strange look on her face. "What is it, Princess?" asked Nettie.

Icya looked away from Nettie and said, "Nothing, it's nothing. Nettie, I am going to lay down for a bit. I'm tired! Thank you for being there for me. I'll call for you when I get up, okay," said Icya, slightly pushing Nettie out of the room.

"Okay, Princess, I'll see you later," replied Nettie.

Icya closed the door and listened to Nettie's footsteps until she could not hear them. Then she gently opened the door, peeped out to make sure no one was in the hallway, and crept down the hall to her father's room. She quietly got close, put her ear on the door and whispered to herself," Ewww, smells like Cotto's armpits! Then with a mildly stern voice, she said, "Father! Father, are you there?" When he did not answer, she cautiously opened the door, went in and closed the door behind her. As soon as she closed the door, she sprinted across the room at full speed to a large chest, opened it and searched around until she found a small, brown pouch. Then she could hear footsteps coming from down the hall. It sounded like more than one person. She put the pouch down through the front of her dress into her underwear and hopped inside the large chest. Congion and Mama Yewande came into the room.

"So the Mwehu powder worked?" asked Mama Yewande.

"Yes, wonderfully," replied Congion.

"How can you say it worked with such bold confidence, when no dead man has appeared upon your doorstep? How can you be so sure?" asked Mama Yewande.

"I dwell in the thoughts and nightmares of one who is very close to King O'Saka. He is mine to control. For him there is no escaping my grasp," said Congion.

"Aye, so you have been in contact with Sheshon, and he knows that his daughter is alive and well," said Mama Yewande, with a smirk on her face.

"Yes! And if he wants her to remain so, he will continue to do as I ask of him. I told you one day she would be useful," replied Congion.

"Do you ever plan to let her return to Ardhi Anasa?" asked Mama Yewande.

"Of course not! Why would I? She knows nothing of her family in Ardhi Anasa. Ever since she was a child, she has served me. She has no desire to leave the kingdom. As long as she remains here, I will always be one step ahead of the beloved King O'Saka and, besides, she's a far better cook than you'll ever be," the evil voodoo king replied.

"Well, that may be true, but there are far more things that a king hungers for than food," said Mama Yewande as she ran her hand down Congion's chest.

"Ewww," whispered Icya as she changed herself into a white mouse, crawled cautiously out of the top of the chest, and crept out of the room with great stealth.

Chapter XVI

Something Doesn't Smell Right

One year had gone by and for some reason Icya had never told Nettie what she had heard in her father's room. One morning, Icya arose, got dressed and went searching through the castle for Nettie because she was hungry. For some reason lately, the servants had been somewhat scarce. "Nettie, Nettie, where are you?" called Icya. Then she could hear footsteps coming closer to her, but she did not see anyone. "Who is that?" she asked.

"It is me, Princess. What do you need?" asked Nettie, looking a little ruffled and reeking of Cotto.

"Nettie, where is he?" asked Icya with rage in her eyes. "Who are you talking about, my Princess," replied the servant nervously.

"You know doggone well of whom I'm speaking! Cotto, where is he?" she demanded.

"I ... I don't know, Princess Icya," she replied, looking more nervous than ever.

"Tell me now," commanded Icya, raising up her hand palm first in front of Nettie's face and gritting her teeth. " Tell me or I will turn you into a piece of bacon as hungry as I am!"

"Okay ... okay, please don't do that! He was here earlier, but that was a couple of hours ago," said Nettie.

"You're lying!" said Icya. "I swear," replied Nettie, looking nervously towards the end of the hallway. Icya noticed her gaze, then started opening every room door until lo and behold it was Cotto. She looked at him with death in her eyes and raised up her hand, looked back at Nettie and with a few choice ancient words turned Nettie into a big, fat pig. Nettie the pig went running off, while Icya turned her gaze back towards Cotto.

Cotto stood about six-foot-five with a dark complexion and light grey eyes. His body was full of perfectly chiseled muscles. By any standard, he was a very attractive man, slash murderous one-eyed monster with some big bat wings at nighttime.

"Princess," he said, standing there with his chest poked out and looking down to the side with a smirk on his face.

"Look, I don't know why my father has summoned you here to our home but, while you are here, you will respect my house," said Icya, covering her nose and making sure not to get too close to him.

The stench that radiated from Cotto's body had certain pheromones that made him more attractive to women than he already was. Some straight men had warned other men to cover their noses if they were ever standing next to him in conversation. He did not discriminate.

"Oh! Is that right? I could have sworn this was the house of Congion, the great voodoo king, but I haven't seen him around much lately," said Cotto, casually walking towards Icya.

"Back the hell up," she yelled as she raised her hand, poised to defend herself or cast another spell. But before she could do anything, he grabbed her by the arm and neck. Then he slammed her against the wall.

"It is good that he is not around! You and I needed some alone time anyway," he said, trying to kiss her.

"Get off of me!" she yelled, struggling to push him away. "Why? Do you want to go play with your little friends the prince and his monkey," he replied.

Fishing for information, she said, "I don't know what you're talking about."

Then he, not being the brightest person in the world, said to her, "I followed you one morning and saw you going through the portal. I've been paying their little kingdom a visit ever since. Yes, and I've really caught an interest in the slant-eyed girl." Then all of a sudden, he lost his footing, slipped down and hit his head on the floor. Icya had conjured up a spell to turn him into a snake, but her spells did not really work that well yet on magical creatures or demons, so it just turned his legs into a snake's tail for a minute, then his legs returned to normal.

Walking out of the room, Icya said, "You will pay for that, you skunk bat." Now Icya was in her room pacing back and forth, still hungry and, for good reason, still worried about Saka and her other friends. She heard some rustling under her bed and looked to see what it was. It was the pig formerly known as Nettie. She looked at her and laughed a little, then turned her back to her normal self. Nettie looked down at herself and started screaming.

"Why did you do that?" she yelled.

"Don't lie to me ever again and, when you see Cotto, you better run!"

"Yes, my Princess. Thank you! Thank you! Thank you," said Nettie, groveling on her knees before Icya.

"And if I smell him on you, I'll turn you into a slug and leave you like that. Have you seen the twins today?" asked Icya.

"No, I haven't seen them in awhile, my Princess," she replied.

"What about Mama Yewande?" asked Icya.

"No, Princess," she answered. "Now go and prepare me some breakfast. I'm hungry!" yelled Icya.

An hour or so had passed and Nettie had not brought the food that Icya requested.

"What in God's name is going on?" said Icya as she got up from her vanity seat and went down the torch-lit hallway towards the kitchen. When she got to the kitchen, there was no one there, but it smelled as if someone had just been cooking.

The kitchen was huge with a firepit in the far right corner and a water well in the center. Pots and pans were hanging from the ceiling over a large wooden island, and the floor was made of stone, covered in black tar. The walls were wood covered in plaster to look like stone. "Nettie!" she yelled, but there was no answer. "This place is going to hell," she said as she grabbed a pot hanging above her and some eggs from a basket. Beside the basket of eggs, she noticed a tray with some strawberries, grapes, a small loaf of pita bread, some grits and some bacon. She tore off a piece of pita bread, grabbed a slice of bacon and shoved it into her mouth.

She stood there and ate half of the food that was on the tray, then walked over to a cupboard to get a cup. As soon as she got in arm's reach of the cupboard, she tripped over something, fell down and hurt her knee. For a while, she sat there with her eyes closed, rubbing her knee. After a minute or two, she opened one eye to see what she had tripped over. She had stumbled over someone's arm. It was Nettie, and she was either dead or unconscious. Icya got and grabbed her.

"Nettie, are you okay? Wake up, girl!" yelled Icya. Now she could smell Cotto's stink, and Nettie's neck was turned almost all the way around to the back. "He killed you!

That murderous freak," Icya screamed as she sat on the ground, holding Nettie to her bosom.

"What's the matter, child?" said Mama Yewande as she walked into the kitchen.

"He killed her," said Icya as tears ran down her face. "Oh my, who killed her, child?" asked Mama Yewande with a truly unconcerned, tired look on her face. "Cotto! Who else?" screamed Icya.

"Calm down, my dear. You really mustn't become so attached to the help," said Mama Yewande, putting her arms around Icya.

"What do you mean? She was a beautiful person with a beautiful soul. She did not deserve to die like this. He just violated her and threw her in the bread closet as if she was nothing. Stop! Get off of me," yelled Icya as she pushed Mama Yewande away from her and got up. "Where is my father?" demanded Icya, standing firmly with one hand on her hip.

"He is busy below. He does not need to be bothered Now, child. I will take care of this, and I will speak with him later," replied Mama Yewande.

"No, I will speak to him now," said Icya as she stormed out of the room.

"Come back here, girl," screamed Mama Yewande with a hateful stare as she stood and watched Icya exit the room.

Chapter XVII

Incwadi Endala

Crying uncontrollably, Icya walked down the long, underlit hallway. She saw someone walking in front of her very slowly, with his or her head down. She could not recognize who it was, but she was curious to find out where they were going so she followed them. After she got a little closer, she could tell this person was a man and that by the way he walked, he was either sick or badly wounded. He smelled dreadfully unpleasant, like a dead person.

His clothes were old and very dirty, and he left a grassy, slimy trail. She continued to follow him, and soon he came upon the back stairwell and proceeded to go down. The stairs were very old and noisy when used.

She would not be able to continue her pursuit unnoticed, so she speedily chanted a very few words and changed herself into a ferret. The stairwell went down at least one hundred steps and the farther down they went, the hotter it got. Once the man reached the bottom of the stairs, he just stopped and stood there, like he was waiting on something or someone. Icya waited just up the stairway, so she couldn't be seen.

About thirty minutes went by and the man just stood there rocking back and forth, while Icya patiently stayed hidden until she could feel the faint vibration of footsteps on the stairs. The vibration slowly turned into definite footsteps. Looking up through the stairwell, Icya could see that it was Mama Yewande, so Icya, the ferret, made her way farther down the stairs.

At the end of the stairs, there was a hall directly in front of the stairs, a hall to the right, and a hall to the left. As soon as she got down to the bottom, she turned left at the man's feet and waited there. Now Mama Yewande could see the man, so she yelled, "Who is that down there?" but the man didn't answer. Mama Yewande kept walking down and asked again,

"Who is down there?" The man just continued in his silence, rocking back and forth like a drunk person. Mama Yewande began to walk faster until she got down to the bottom. She then grabbed him by his shoulders and said, "Aya! You made it. Then she grabbed him by the chin, lifted up his head, and studied his face. Up against the wall hidden in the shadows about five feet away, Icya can now see by his eyes that this man has no soul but, more importantly, this man is dead. His face was half-eaten, and the grassy, sludgelike mixture from the trail he left was actually coming out of his mouth.

After Mama Yewande looked at him for a minute or two, she grabbed him by the arm and took him with her through the hallway directly in front of the stairs. Icya, with much skill, stayed in the shadows, crossed to the other side, and followed them to another set of stairs. This one went down about fifty steps. Now, it was hot enough to cause an instant sweat.

At the bottom of the stairs, Mama Yewande took the man down the right hallway, all the way to the end that opened up into a gigantic underground cavern with candles lit everywhere. Icya could also see Congion, the twins and two other men sitting in a large circle with their eyes closed, chanting evil incantations. Over and over again, they chanted.

Mama Yewande took the man to Congion, who was standing on the outside of the circle with his back towards the circle. An unconscious elderly woman lay on a table in front of him, and Congion stood behind an altar as if he was about to preach a great sermon. He grabbed the man by the chin, studied his face, and pulled a knife from his robe. Then he stepped from behind the altar towards the woman, sliced her throat and let the blood flow into a saucepan.

Terrified from what she saw, Icya screamed, but the scream of a ferret is more like a long chirp. No one noticed. Now Icya was shaking heavily with her eyes bucked and locked on the bleeding woman that her father had just now murdered. Mama Yewande promptly took her place in the circle. Slowly,

Congion picked up the blood-filled saucepan, looked down inside the pan, swished it around, and then tossed the blood into the middle of the circle.

Before the blood hit the ground, it changed its color five times, from red to black to fluorescent pink, then back to black and to red again. When the blood hit the ground, it instantly burned a hole that had to reach to the depths of hell, because a fire came up from the hole with a demon trapped inside it. Congion looked at the demon, and the demon looked back as if he knew him. Then, suddenly, Congion grabbed the dead man by the top of his head and pulled him closer to the circle.

He then reached his other hand out until it was inside the circle, regained eye contact with the demon and began to invoke the evil spirits. The fire burned hotter and hotter and higher and higher.

Now as Congion struggled to pull his hand out of the circle, a trail of black fire and smoke stretched from the big fire to his hand. As soon as that hand was completely outside the circle, he put it on the man's head and put the other hand inside the circle. Instantaneously, the demon took possession of the man, raised his head towards Congion, and opened his jet- black, tormented eyes.

Suddenly, the demon noticed another demon in the fire trying to escape, so then he raised his hand, pointed at it, started screaming a horrible, high-pitched, squealing, scraping sound but was still looking directly into Congion's eyes. Congion then struggled to turn his eyes and head away from the possessed man back toward the demon trying to escape from the fire. The second he regained eye contact with the demon in the fire, it passed through him onto the man, and then another and then another.

The more that came, the faster they came until there were thousands of demons passing through Congion and possessing the dead man by the minute. Now, Congion was floating and pulsating in midair, with one hand stuck to the head of the dead man and the other still inside the circle drawing demons out of the fire. Now with his entire body fully engulfed in black flames and smoke, the chanting elevated. The cavern was filled with the sound of ripping wind coming from miniature tornados that had formed around the circle. For each person in the circle, there was a very small tornado. These inconceivable acts of evil carried on for close to an hour while Icya watched in horror.

Now unconscious, Congion was an open gateway from hell for endless amounts of hell's minions to squad up here on earth. There seemed to be no stopping this invading force until Cotto suddenly appeared from the shadows.

"You will be the death of us both, you fool," said Cotto as he grabbed Congion by the hands and pulled one hand out of the circle and the other from the head of the overly possessed dead man. Now holding Congion in one hand, he pushed the body of the dead woman off the table and gently laid Congion on it. All of the miniature tornadoes were spinning a lot faster than they were before, and they were moving closer to each person in the circle. Then all of a sudden, a tornado sucked one of the men in and tossed him in the fire to a crispy-fried death. The other tornadoes were pulling demon spirits that had escaped the fire but went into one of the people in the circle instead. The demons were all screaming trying to go back into the humans, but they could not escape the pull of the twisting tornadoes.

After that, the small whirl winds went into the fire and seemed to extinguish it.

The demon-possessed man was screaming, still pointing towards the center of the circle with his eyes locked on Congion, until Cotto got in its face and asked the demon, "What is your name?" The vessel immediately stopped screaming, looked Cotto directly in the eyes and promptly admitted his gaze to the ground.

"I am Legion," he replied in a voice that sounded like an out-of-tune evil church choir.

"Who am I?" asked Cotto.

"You are Popobawa, third in command of the entire realm of hell, with dominion over many legions," he replied as the skin fell from his fiery red, illuminating skeleton face. "We are yours to command, my master," said Legion.

"Get up," said Cotto in a low and calm voice. Legion just looked at him. Then the recently sacrificed woman got up and stood in front of Cotto, still dripping blood from her neck. "And what may I ask is your name?" said Cotto.

"My name is Ngono. I am Kulevya. We are here to serve you, master," the demon inside the woman replied, gazing down at the breast and legs of the woman's body it has possessed with the look of what seemed to be amazement. "And serve me you shall."

Everyone in the room was unconscious except Icya and Legion. Icya patiently waited in stealth for a time to leave. Congion grabbed the possessed woman by her bloody neck, threw her off into a dark corner and disappeared into that corner. Legion just stood there and watched until Cotto said,

"What are you doing just standing there? Look at all these able bodies. You just got out. Go and get you some." Legion went straight for Congion. "Stop! Not that one. Go have your way with the tall one there, Mama Yewande, " said Cotto, smirking to the side, but then he saw Congion trying to wake up and said, "No! Stop! Take that guy." Legion pointed to the only man in the circle and Cotto said, "Yeah, that guy."

Icya saw that they have occupied themselves, so she took this chance to scuttle back upstairs and get back to the kitchen to see if Nettie's body was still there, but it was gone. When she got back to her room, she began to cry, screaming at the top of her lungs.

"I have to leave this wicked place tonight!" she said under her breath as she packed a few clothes, books, candles and some other small things. She then placed everything that she had packed under her bed and began to flip through the pages of different books that were still on her shelf. Every so often, she ripped out the pages, folding them and collecting them together. She went on tearing out pages for hours until it was right before dark. When she was done, she placed the collection of pages, which were a mixture of spells, incantations, rituals and medicine notes, along with what she had packed earlier. Then she opened her door and peeped out to see if anyone was in the hall, turned herself into the white mouse and went crawling down the hall. The hallway was empty, so she raced along the wall and stayed in the shadows until she got to the back stairwell. She went down the first set of stairs, then the next until she came upon the dungeon.

Congion and Mama Yewande were probably still in his room, and the twins were most likely laid up somewhere with Cotto, but the sun was almost down so they would be back soon. Icya returned to her normal form and ran to the altar (the last place she saw the Incwadi Endala, the Dark Grimoires), the oldest and most powerful collection of rituals and spells known to man that she had now, regrettably, stolen from King O'Saka. She looked on, in and around the altar, but it was not there. "Where is it? It has to be here somewhere," she whispered to herself.

Frustrated and disappointed, she walked back up the stairs, then changed into the mouse, On her way to her room, she passed by Congion's room as he and Mama Yewande were coming out and, to her dismay, Congion was carrying the Dark Grimoires cuffed in his left hand. She waited along the wall in the shadows for a while, then carefully followed them back down to the dungeon.

When she finally made it back down the stairs, Congion was at the altar with the book open, chanting. Mama Yewande was sitting in the circle, Indian-style, repeating after him. This went on for a while until they were both repeating the words in unison. Then Congion left the altar and joined Mama Yewande in the circle. Now both Congion and Mama

Yewande's eyes were closed and in a deep trance, so Icya crawled over to the altar, got behind it, crawled up the altar, stood on top of the book, turned herself into the peregrine falcon, grabbed the book in her talons, and flew out of the dungeon towards the stairwell. She got all the way up the stairs, only to fly right by Apunda and Yejide on their way down.

"Aya," said the twins in unison.

'Then Apunda said, "Go tell mama," changed herself into a bird and flew off after Icya. Yejide went running down to the dungeon to inform Mama Yewande that a bird had flown off with the Dark Grimoires. Icya swiftly flew and when she got close to her room door, she transformed to herself in midair, rolled one time when she hit the ground, and when she came out of the roll, she was on her feet opening her room door. Apunda was coming up behind her fast so she slammed the door and locked it. Apunda crashed into the door, knocking herself unconscious and falling to the floor.

Meanwhile, Congion, Mama Yewande and Yejide were running up the hallway. Icya grabbed her things from under the bed, hopped onto the bed and started chanting. Now Congion was beating on the door trying to get in but, when he did, Icya had disappeared with the Dark Grimoires safely tucked under her arm. As soon as she came out of the portal, she sealed it and ran to the next one. After she passed through the portal, she sealed that one, collapsed to her knees and started crying. When she regained her composure, she cloaked herself in fog and mist, then moved like the wind until she got to the Victoria River. The boat that had carried her across before was waiting on her. She got aboard, and it carried her across again.

As soon as she got to the other side, she began to move swiftly through the forest as if she was walking on air. For hours, she traveled until she reached a little village called Mwana. She had a lot of relatives in Mwana with whom she could hide out for a little while until she could figure out what to do.

Back in Shetani, Congion had summoned the beast Popobawa and had ordered him to find Icya and bring her and the book back, but when Popobawa realized that the portal had been sealed, he was forced to make a two-day journey to Ardhi Anasa.

Chapter XVIII

Sazi

A little more than a week has passed since Icya escaped from the house of Congion. About fifteen miles north of Ardhi Anasa palace in the small village of Mwana (birthplace of Queen Nidera, Mama Yewande and Solange), people are being abducted and families are terrified to be outside in the night. In pursuit of Icya, the menacing bat-winged creature Popobawa within a week's time had crippled the small community and for one family in particular (the Chokowes), life has become one horrific nightmare after another.

Meanwhile, on the other side of the village, Icya was well-rested but feeling responsible for the terrible things the monster had done while looking for her, so she decided to leave her slightly older cousin Abena's house to try to talk to Saka. Assuring her cousin and her children that the danger would soon be over, Icya bought a horse, loaded up her stuff and said her goodbyes. She then headed out for Nakuru Village, where she could rent a room.

Two nights ago, Bonte (an eighteen-year-old, the oldest son of the Chokowe family) went to the vegetable market to get some seed to plant and a couple of things for the household. There was about two full hours of brilliant sunlight left, and the 99market was just ten minutes away. Bonte's mother, Sazi, insisted that he wait for his father, Gelmy, to return from work. He actually worked at the meat market, about twenty feet from the same vegetable market that Bonte was going to, but Bonte had ulterior motives. He wanted to go see his lady friend who resided about fifteen minutes past the markets. So instead of going straight home after he left the market, he went to see her.

After he got there, he lost track of time, and it was getting dark before he noticed. When he started to leave, the parents of his lady friend asked him to stay because of the people who had been abducted in the last week. He told them that he would rather go home because his parents would be worried and would probably go out and look for him.

He left and when he did not return home that night, his parents were understandingly worried, so Gelmy went to see if he could find him. He went by the young woman's house and was told that his son was asked to stay but had left a long time ago. Gelmy stayed out all night until the sun came up. When he got home, he kissed his wife and left again. This time, he formed a search party of about twenty men, horses and bloodhounds. They looked all day until the sun went down, then all of the other men went home to their families, but Gelmy stayed out looking for Bonte. Sazi, his wife, and Trecie and Rishi, his other two children, waited patiently at home for their Bonte and Gelmy to return that night, but neither of them did.

The next morning, Sazi went to go talk to the village elders about her husband and son to see if they would form another search party to go look for them. The elders decided to do what she asked, and they looked until nightfall but did not find them. They told her they would search again tomorrow, and they did.

The next day, about five hours into the search, they found Gelmy dead deep in the forest and brought his body back to the now-widowed Sazi. She and their children were devastated by his death, but she felt there was still hope for her beloved son Bonte. She begged the elders to go out and look for one more day, but the elders told her that her son was most likely dead and that they had to use their resources to search for a couple of women who were missing since last night. She went about asking men to help her look for her boy, but all of the men said almost the exact same words that the elders had said. So she decided to wait till the next morning and she and the children would go looking.

The next morning, she arose, got the children ready, put Rishi her youngest child in a wrap on her back, and tied a small rope from her hand to the hand of Trecie, her eight-year- old daughter.

Before they set out to search, Sazi decided to go feed the animals in the small barn before they left because they would probably be gone all day. When she opened the door of the barn, she noticed that the animals were uneasy or even a little frightened. She looked around but did not see anything unusual, but she could smell a strange scent mixed in with the usual animal smell. She looked around a little more and then cautiously walked over to a bin where they kept the chicken feed, grabbed a scoop and bent down to get some feed.

The bin was close to a large pile of hay. She scooped the feed and tossed some to the chickens. Then as she attempted to scoop a second time, a hand grabbed her from the pile of hay. She screamed as he slung her and her children to the ground. A shirtless Cotto with ripped, bloody pants emerged from the pile of hay. He stood over them with an evil, murderous look in his eyes and a rotten smile on his face. Now both of the children were frightened and screaming, but Sazi had suddenly calmed down. The pheromones had now saturated her lungs, and she was nearly helpless to the toxins circulating through her bloodstream, but Sazi somehow got up, grabbed Trecie and ran out of the barn into the house. Cotto just stood there and watched them until they went into the house, and then he walked to the barn door and shut it.

Now in the house, Sazi and the children were sitting at a table in their small kitchen. Trecie was still crying and asking her mother questions, but Sazi was not saying anything. She was just sitting in the chair, holding Rishi and staring towards the barn, occasionally looking at Trecie and sweating profusely. Eventually after an hour had gone by and both of the children had gone to sleep, Sazi got up, put the kids in their bed and walked to the window adjacent to the barn. She gradually pulled the curtain back with the arm that Cotto had grabbed her by and peeked out, only to see that the barn door was wide open and Cotto was staring back at her. His scent was still on her arm, and the effect of the toxins from his touch had reignited something deep within her. She quickly closed the curtain, walked back to her chair and sat down, breathing heavily.

Sitting there with her arms folded and looking up at the ceiling with tears in her eyes, she glanced down at her arm, pulled it up to her nose, closed her eyes, and took a long, deep inhale. Her hand then continued up to her head. She stroked her hair and grabbed it firmly before sprinting to the kids' room to check on them. Then Sazi quietly closed the door, locked it, turned around with her bottom lip trembling in uncontrollable lust, and dashed out of the house towards the barn. Running as fast as she can, she leaped onto Cotto and wrapped her arms and legs around him. Cotto smiled and shut the door behind them.

Hours passed and it was about twenty minutes before sundown. Trecie woke up and called for her mother, but Sazi was still in the barn. She got up and looked at her little brother.

He was still sound asleep, so she went in the kitchen where she last saw her mother, looked around the house and called out for her again, but she got no answer. Now scared and confused, she grabbed the wrap that her mother used to carry Rishi, went to the room, and with all her strength secured him on her back. Cautiously, she walked to the window and peeped out, hoping her mother would come any minute, but she did not, so Trecie decided to go outside to look for her. Trecie very slowly opened the front door and looked out towards the barn.

Now the sun had gone down and nightfall had cast its dark shadow across the land. In the whole village, Trecie is the only soul who dared to step out into the darkness. First, she went around to the back of the house to see if her mother might be hanging clothes on the line or pulling them off the line, but she was not there.

Her last choice was to check the barn but, as she walked towards the barn, she could hear a terrible noise that sounded like a woman, a man and a big grizzly bear screaming in excruciating agony while being beaten in the throat with a large wooden stick. The beating sound started out slowly, but then it got faster and faster and faster until it turned into a rumbling sound along with the terrible screaming.

Inside the barn, a horrific transformation was taking place. Cotto was floating in midair over Sazi's beaten and torn body. His head had tripled in size, and his mouth tore from ear to ear, filling up with long, skinny, razor-sharp teeth. The air around him was twisting and twirling, circling his now-deformed body like a small tornado. The back of his neck was stretching and pulling the skin on his back, ripping a hole. Then his arms started to retract back into his arm sockets and from the hole in his back protruded some larger arms attached to enormous wings.

While the wings were forming, everything got silent until he raised both of them high above his head and in one big flap, booooom! From a thunderous and powerful blast of wind and light, the front of the barn was blown to pieces, and his transformation was complete.

He screamed a long and horrible scream as he grabbed the near-dead Sazi with his long, wretched feet and with a flap of his wings knocked down the rest of the half-destroyed barn and flew off into the night sky. Poor Trecie was helpless as she witnessed in terror the horrifying abduction of her beautiful and loving mother, Sazi.

Chapter XIX

Epic Surprises

Three years had passed since anyone had seen or heard from Mykail after disappearing into the rain forest. King O'Saka frequently asked about her, still under the impression that she's a he. Saka just told him that he did not know where he was, never revealing what actually happened. Thundar went searching for her about a dozen times but never so much as picked up her scent. It was very strange to all of them.

Saka and Thundar were both turning eighteen in two days. There was usually a huge celebration for an occasion as such but not this year. King O'Saka had decided to hold off on the big parties until he felt everything was safe. Instead, he decided to expose Saka to the power of the amulets. The King, Nakatu and Thundar had thoroughly tested the limits of the amulets. No harm had come to them in the years of their use, except for a few bits of extreme tiredness, so King O'Saka felt it was time. The next morning, Saka and Thundar were up getting dressed and preparing for their daily lessons. Saka opened up the balcony overlooking Treazur Lake.

"Haha! Look at Zolatar and Volaris. They are forever running around chasing each other. I wonder what Father has planned for us," said the Prince, still gazing towards the master rhino.

"Hrrhuur," grunted Thundar, shrugging his shoulders.

"So, brother, you are like thirty-two in gorilla years."

"Aye! You're getting old, man," said Saka, jokingly. Then he hopped on Thundar's back, and they started wrestling all over the room. They were throwing each other down and bumping into the walls so hard that one of the guards burst in to check on the commotion.

"Is everything okay, my Prince?" asked the guard. Saka and Thundar paused for a second from tussling on the floor, looked at the guard and laughed.

Saka told the man, "Come quick, my leg is hurt." The guard hurried to him. Saka then grabbed the guard, picked him up over his head and looked at Thundar and smiled. Meanwhile, the man was begging Saka to put him down and was trying his best to get loose, but Saka was so strong now. The guard was utterly helpless.

Then Saka asked Thundar, "Should I put him down?" Thundar shook his head no, then Saka reared back and threw the guard at least ten feet towards his enormous bed. Before the guard hit the bed, both Saka and Thundar were airborne, legs first, parallel to each other. In midair with Thundar on the left and Saka on the right, they grabbed each other's right hands and rotated to opposite sides. As they came down, Saka yelled, "Flying leg drop!" As soon as the guard hit the middle of the bed, Saka and Thundar came down on top of him with the backs of their legs. Their knees were slightly bent so that they did not hurt the guard. Boom! The bed collapsed to the ground. For a second, the guard just laid there scared to death, then he hopped up and ran out of the room, cursing and bumping into Zulin.

Zulin stood smiling in the doorway. She was breathtaking with a beauty unmatched by anyone in the kingdom, young or old. Her jet-black hair flowed flawlessly all the way down to her perfectly shaped calf muscles. She was Oriental, but the African sun had graciously tanned her skin to a golden bronze. And the makeup she wore radiantly enhanced her features: green shimmering eyeliner with light blue neonlike lipstick. The dress she had on matched her makeup in color and shimmer. It was skin-tight from the neck down, hugging her dangerous curves, then at the knees, it loosened into a frontal drape the color of her skin complexion.

"What did you do to him?" she asked.

"Aww nothing, he was more scared than hurt. We were just fooling around," said the Prince.

"Well, are you going to finish getting dressed?" Zulin asked softly.

"Oh right," said the Prince, grabbing his shirt hurriedly. "You know what? You should just walk around with no shirt on all day. I wouldn't mind," said Zulin as she smiled and posed with her hand on her hip.

"I bet you wouldn't, you freaky old lady," replied Saka. Then he ran towards her, picked her up and gently brought her down to his lips, and they kissed with ample passion.

"I love you, my Prince," said Zulin, looking deep into Saka's eyes.

"I love you more," replied Saka, simultaneously slapping her on the butt.

"Oww! Come on. Let's go," said Zulin.

"You look amazing, but why are you dressed like that?" asked Saka.

"I've come to tell you that father has canceled lessons today," replied Zulin.

"Why?" asked the Prince.

"He gave me no reason," she answered.

"Oh well, I guess you can walk me to my early morning class then," said Saka.

"Okay," she replied. All of them walked to the classrooms but found out that everything had been canceled. Saka and Zulin went on their way, and Thundar went to see the king to find out why they weren't having classes. King O'Saka was in his usual place, the study room. When Thundar found him, he was smoking on a large pipe and strumming elegant notes on the long-neck lute. He appeared to be very deep in thought and was also wearing one of the amulets. Thundar stood in front of him, but the King didn't seem to recognize his presence.

Then he said with a troubled voice, "Why couldn't I have had the amulets before my beloved Nidera was taken from me?" He looked at Thundar with tears in his eyes and said," I could have saved her." Thundar looked at the king with sadness in his eyes and put his hand on his shoulders. Then the king said, "At least out of all the madness, Saka and I found you. Here put the amulet on. Let's talk." Thundar put it on. The light from his eyes was blinding for a few seconds, then it subsided.

"So Father, why are we not in studies today?" asked Thundar.

"As you know, tomorrow is Saka's birthday, but there will be no formal celebration. Instead, we will celebrate the rebirth of Saka's mind," the King pronounced.

"So you plan to introduce Saka to the amulets' power tomorrow?" asked Thundar.

"Yes. I have amassed vast amounts of knowledge and endless amounts of wealth using the amulets. Now it is my son's turn to reap the ascended blessings of Yeshua. Nakatu says he is sure that you have no equal in hand-to-hand combat and that in the use of the javelin, you are without flaw. He says he can teach you nothing more. With my guidance and the amulets' essence, I will teach both of you to harness this power and sync your minds together to fight as one," said King O'Saka with great vigor in his voice.

"This is wonderful news, Father. I am eager to train with my brother and master the plan you speak of," said Thundar, grunting and inflating his cheeks in excitement and trying to keep his composure. Thundar returned the amulet to the king and went searching for Saka, but it took awhile to find him.

In the meantime, the Prince and Zulin were in her room making out. The two of them were madly in love, and both of them wanted desperately to make love, but Saka believed and was taught that the longer people saved themselves before marriage, the stronger they would be in life. He stopped them every time they got too close. That took a lot of willpower. This frustrated Zulin, but most of the time she took it well.

Thud, Thud, Thud!

"Who is it?" yelled Zulin. "Hrrhuur!" replied Thundar.

"I'm coming, brother," said Saka as he got up, kissed Zulin and opened the door.

"What is it, brother?" asked Saka. Thundar told him what his father had said, and Thundar went to prepare for an indefinite trip. In the meantime, Saka and Zulin were back locking lips.

About thirty minutes passed and Zulin said to Saka, "So what did Thundar want?"

"He told me that we are leaving tomorrow for a long trip and that I should pack my things," replied Saka.

"Tomorrow!" shouted Zulin. "Yeah," replied the Prince.

"But tomorrow is your birthday. I had something special planned for you," Zulin said regrettably.

"I kind of knew you would. I'm sorry, Zulin, but Father says it is very important, so I must go," replied Saka, pulling her closer to him. She pulled away from him and asked, "But for how long?"

"I do not know. Thundar didn't know, either," he answered. Then there was a knock at the door.

"Zulin," called a strong voice.

"Yes, father," replied Zulin.

"Come, I need to speak with you," he said. "I need to go anyway," said Saka. "Nooooo," said Zulin with tears in her eyes. "Zulin," her dad called again.

"I'm coming. I'll see you later?" she asked.

"Okay, sweetness," replied Saka as he got up, walked out and said hello to her father.

Meanwhile, in Nakuru Village, Icya had rented a room, settled in and was getting some needed rest after the long journey.

With everything that had been happening around her, she did not realize that Saka's birthday had already come around again and that they planned to leave for Hazina early in the morning.

Later, back at the palace, Saka and Thundar were in their room getting ready.

"Do you know where we are going?" asked Saka. Thundar shook his head no.

"We are going somewhere special to train," signed Thundar.

"Me and you?" asked Saka. Thundar excitedly nodded his head yes.

"I'm excited too, brother," said Saka, smiling. "Thundar, do you ever think about Mykail, if that was even his or her name?" Saka asked.

"Sometimes," signed Thundar.

"Well, I'm done packing. I'll see you later," said Saka as he raced out the door back to Zulin.

Later on that evening, in her room, Zulin told the Prince that the reason her dad wanted to speak to her was to let her know that he would be leaving also, along with them. She also showed Saka a beautiful diamond-tipped knife that her father had given her. After that, they talked for a while and fell asleep in each other's arms.

The next morning before sunrise, Icya got out of bed, dressed herself and headed out towards the palace to maybe get a glimpse of Prince Saka. In the form of the falcon, she flew over the courtyard and noticed Zolatar and Volaris, both harnessed to a large carriage that resembled a boat. There were three smaller carriages and about one hundred soldiers with horses, all preparing to go somewhere. She perched herself onto a branch right over the heads of two soldiers talking so she could hear what they were saying. They weren't saying anything of interest, so she decided to sneak into the palace. As soon as the front door of the palace was clear, she swooped down to the ground close to the entrance, changed to the white mouse and scurried inside. Then she hurried to King O'Saka's study room.

King O'Saka, Master Yasufe, Saka, Thundar, Zulin, General Nakatu and the five elders met in the king's study. The king left the kingdom in the hands of the five elders until the royal family returned. King O'Saka still gave no date that they would return, but he did discuss the path that they were taking.

When Icya realized that Saka was about to leave on an indefinite trip, she ran out of the study and out of the palace, then changed back into the bird and swiftly headed back to her room. She had to hurry to gather her things and load them on her horse if she was going to catch up with them. Meanwhile, everyone back at the palace said their goodbyes while Zolatar and Volaris anxiously waited outside.

"Okay, let's go!" shouted King O'Saka. They left in a grand caravan. About an hour had passed and no one had said a word until Saka asked.

"So, Father, exactly where are we going?"

"Wouldn't you like to know? It is a surprise. Do not worry. You're gonna love it," he replied.

Later that night, they stopped to set up camp after crossing the Victoria River. The king told Prince Saka what he and Thundar had been up to and what he had planned for them. He showed them a book that he had written with detailed training specifically for them. He explained to Saka how the amulets worked and how he would give them to him in the very near future. Saka was so excited to hear this amazing news. After they finished talking, Saka and Thundar went off to themselves and Thundar continued filling him in on what had been going on. The two boys conversed until they fell asleep.

Meanwhile, several miles behind them, Icya raced to catch up with them, cloaked in fog to avoid detection by soldiers or the monster Popobawa. After she crossed the Victoria River, she could see the smoke from their campfires about a mile away, so she got off her horse, took her things and walked the rest of the way. Soon, she came upon a few of the soldiers and the carriage that Master Yasufe and General Nakatu were traveling in.

At this time, no one was inside the carriage, but there were too many men close by to put her things aboard without detection. For about an hour, she waited in the cloak of darkness for the right moment. Campfires were lit all around, and the carriage shone like the morning sun. A diversion seemed like the right choice, but she really didn't have much time, so she sat down, got some bread out of one of her bags, ate a piece and then closed her eyes to meditate.

About ten minutes had passed and all of a sudden a ringing noise broke her out of her meditation. It was a dinner bell and, when she opened her eyes, all of the men were gone.

"Thank you, Yeshua," she said as she grabbed her things, carefully made her way to the carriage and hid her bags and herself among the luggage. Tired from a very long and trying day, she fell asleep with a slight smile of contentment on her face.

The next morning, everyone packed up and continued on the journey. Only an hour had passed when one of the men on horseback in front yelled, "Stop!"

"Oh my goodness, why are we stopping?" yelled the King.

"There is something blocking the path and there is no way around it," replied the man.

"Well, knock it down or move it out the way!" shouted the King, more agitated than expected.

"What's wrong, Father?" asked Saka.

"This is very close to where we lost your mother. It was about one hundred feet in that direction from this very spot. This is also where we found you, Thundar. This place brings back a range of memories. Anyway, how are you coming with the removal of, what is it anyway?" shouted the King.

"Looks like a large rock, sire," replied one man. It was as big as twenty men and oval in shape. One of the men put his foot on it to test its weight. As soon as his foot pressed against the structure, his whole leg broke inside and made a big hole in it. "Break it down," he said. Some of the men started kicking and chopping at it with their swords and axes.

After ten minutes of battering the object, the only additional damage to it was another hole the same shape and size as the first. For a minute, King O'Saka just stood there and stared at the large object. Eventually, he walked up to it and examined the structure thoroughly. He bent down and looked into one of the holes. His entire body could fit inside the hole easily. Very discreetly, he picked up something from inside the object and put it in his pocket.

"Grab some rope, make a noose between the two holes and attach it to the master rhino," said King O'Saka. Now the structure was hooked to Zolatar and Volaris. The King yelled, "Pull Zo, pull Vola!" The massive animals started unearthing a sight much more enormous and frightening than anyone could have ever imagined.

First what they thought was maybe a big rock turned out to be a gigantic head. As the master rhino continued to pull, they next unearthed the giant neck, chest, legs, and feet of the biggest man skeleton that anyone had ever seen in a nightmare. It had to be at least thirty feet tall. Back in the carriage of the stowaway, Icya cautiously raised her head and got a glimpse of the amazing scene. Her jaw dropped as she witnessed what the men had unearthed, and then she laid back down with her mouth still wide open.

"What is that, Father?" asked Saka with a concerned and slightly scared look on his face. "That my son is the very intact remains of the ancient race of giant called the Nephlim. Said to be God's first men of the earth, the Nephlim were rulers of the land and sea. They lived for thousands of years in peace. Most of them eventually died of loneliness because there were no Nephlim women. When God realized the reason for their demise, he created smaller versions and he made woman to complete man. The few giants who still roamed the earth became jealous and envious of the life God had made for the small, newer man. They started plotting and became the first kings of man. They tricked man into hating each other for reasons unknown to them, and man soon learned the horrors of war.

Soon there were just two giants left and the new man was tired of their women getting raped and torn to pieces, tired of fighting and perishing for nothing. Therefore, one day when the giants thought they were alone in these woods, the man set large fires a mile away from in a circle around the giants. The fire did not kill them. It was the smoke.

"Sire, what should we do with it?" asked Nakatu. "Leave it. What else can we do with it? We will come back for it," said the King. So they kept traveling for days and on the fifth morning of their travels, the King told the boys about the amount of gold, silver, diamonds and treasure he had acquired over the years. He told them how the amulets gave him the knowledge to understanding where and how such treasures may have the potential to accumulate. He had also learned how to manipulate certain minerals and metals. He told them that the place that he had built was like no place in the world. As he continued to talk to them, a bright light lit up the horizon, but it was not the sun.

The sun was overhead. It was absolutely blinding. "Father, what is that?" asked Saka. "Now that, my beautiful sons, is your kingdom. Hazina!" replied the King. "Thundar, go and tell the others to go ahead. You, Saka and I will be there shortly," said the King. Thundar did as King O'Saka instructed and returned promptly.

The three of them got out of the coach, and King O'Saka pulled a small pouch out of his pocket. Look what I found inside the skull of the Nephlim. Two more power rubies that fit perfectly into the amulets. It is time, my son. I must admit that I am curious to see the wonderful, new power they possess, but my time and the amulets have passed. Happy birthday, my son! Here are the amulets. Put the jewels in them, and put the power amulets on," said the King with great pride in his eyes and chest as he passed them to his sons.

When both of them inserted the power rubies into the slots, a high-pitched humming sound vibrated from them, and the surface exterior of the medallions changed from very smooth to rough.

Now looking at each other, Saka said, "Okay then! Now brother!" This time a great boom like that of a cannon followed the cold and light. When they opened their eyes, Saka just stood there and stared at Thundar because he was at least five feet taller than he was before, and his body was chiseled to perfection with enormous muscles. Even their clothes were bigger.

"**Oh my God,**" said Thundar to Saka in his mind.

"**I can hear you,**" replied Saka telepathically.

"You are enormous, brother!" said Thundar, this time with his mouth and voice to King O'Saka and Saka's surprise.

"What, you can speak now?" asked the King in amazement.

"Yes, Father, I wanted to wait until the right time to show you!" said Thundar with great joy.

"Whoa!" screamed Saka, full of excitement as he slapped the bark of a tree. Wham! The side of the tree practically exploded, and the tree tumbled down towards the King, but Thundar caught it and threw it out of sight.

"Hahahaha!" they all laughed uncontrollably until King O'Saka said, "Okay, calm down, boys. We have to be very careful. This power you have is very dangerous and can never fall into the wrong hands. Come, my sons," said the King.

When they came upon a bridge by a lake, the King said, "My sons, this is your first line of defense. To outsiders, this is the single way in and the only way out of your new kingdom." As they got closer to the gates, the reflection got more unbearable.

"Why and how is the city so bright?" asked Thundar.

"Boys, when the trees are cut down around the city to make way for growth, everyone from hundreds of miles away will be able to see our city. It will act as a beacon to people all over. We will welcome them if they prove an asset; if not, we will train them. If training is not an option, we will take care of the sick and elderly. No one will go hungry, but laziness will not be tolerated. Now, I know that as many who will come to make a life for themselves, more will come to take lives, riches and power for themselves. Well, they will try, but the two Princes will not be allowing any nonsense of that sort. Also, we have been training the grandest army ever assembled.

Fortunes upon fortunes of gold, silver, diamonds and rubies placed on certain rooftops supply the great glimmer that is blinding but impossible to turn away. We will be in full spectacle as soon as the army is fully trained. I now have no doubt that our kingdom is the richest and soon to be the most powerful. It will become the center of the world!" proclaimed the King.

As they got closer, the gates seemed to be made of ivory, wood and silver.

Saka and Thundar could not believe what they saw. Three tall buildings made almost entirely of gold and glass and standing in front of the building stood two giant gold statues of Saka and Thundar standing back to back (Saka drawing his sword and Thundar throwing his spear). "Ohhhhhhhh!" both of them yelled in amazement. However, their voices were so loud and powerful that the ground cracked under Saka's statue and it almost fell down. The sound brought the King to his knees. "Whoa," he said.

"Oh my God! Every part of you has intensified immensely. I wonder what else you can do," said the King with a great big smile on his face. "Go now and look around. Meet me in front of the statues in three hours," said King O'Saka.

"Come on, Thundar, I have to pee," said Saka in a whisper so he would not cause any more damage with his newly discovered super voice. As they walked, they noticed all of the vegetation was enlarged and even the animals were bigger than usual. There were trees, plants and flowers that they had never seen before, but they could name them with one hundred percent accuracy. This place was a fort but paradise at the same time.

By now, people from surrounding villages of the kingdom were showing up. Most were coming to join the army or to find work, and others came to visit but ended up staying. Most of the young men became soldiers and were taught a trade. All of them were terrified at the sight of the Princes.

Meanwhile, on the east side of the city at the soldiers' headquarters, some men were unloading the carriage where Icya hid. Quickly, she changed into the white mouse and crawled into one of her bags. Master Yasufe and General Nakatu had been dropped off at another building to go meet King O'Saka. One of the soldiers grabbed Icya's bags and asked another soldier whose bags they were. Neither knew, so they put them with General Nakatu's things. The soldier took the luggage to General Nakatu's room and closed the door behind him. As soon as Icya heard the door close, she crawled out of the bag and looked around for a minute. The room was nice but relatively empty. She then changed herself into Mykail, grabbed her bags, cracked open the door, and eased out of the building.

When she got out onto the street, it was easy to blend in. There were plenty of people walking around. While walking, she came upon a young man and asked him where someone could rent a room to stay for a long while. The young man pointed her towards an inn where newcomers could stay and find work. It was ten minutes farther east from where she was, so she proceeded to walk, looking around in amazement. This city was like nothing she had ever seen. Most of the people were wearing the same clothing or uniform with the kingdom's insignia on the chest. Buildings were being built all around.

As soon as she reached the inn, she rented a small room on the second floor. It had a bed and was very clean. At the moment, that was all she needed. She unpacked her things, lit a few candles and moved the bed over enough to draw a circle. Then she sat in the circle, meditated and performed a ritual to make another portal. After that was over, she moved the bed back, laid down and went to sleep.

Chapter XX

As One

About a mile away in a large building in the center of the city, the King emerged from a hidden doorway to go to meet the boys. He met them and took them back through the secret passage. They went down on a narrow but sturdy stairway about one hundred feet down. When they got close to the bottom, Thundar said, "I feel a lot of moisture in the air." As soon as he said that, he could see something sparkling ahead of them. But when they stepped out of the stairwell and looked overhead, it looked like large clusters of stars; however, it was not stars. It was blue and red rubies embedded in the ceiling, at least eighty feet high. The moisture they smelled was an enormous underground lake. This place was incredible. There were priceless stones the size of lions bursting out of the wall.

"This is where you will train, my sons," said the King.

"There you are. Ohhh, great lord of lords," said General Nakatu as he fell to his knees in awe of the Prince's great stature. Master Yasufe could not say anything when he saw the boys.

"Master Yasufe, are you okay?" asked Thundar. Master Yasufe's mouth opened wider and his arms dropped lower.

"Oh yeah, that's one detail I failed to inform you about. Thundar can speak."

"Now, show us what you can do. We know that you are strong. Let's see how powerful your legs are," Nakatu said.

Both of them simultaneously burst into the air with so much force and speed that the uptake yanked the others off the ground a little and they fell down. Prince Saka went at least thirty feet into the air, and Thundar went at least twenty feet higher than he did. When Saka hit the ground, he blasted off running like a star shooting across the sky.

"**Catch me, brother**," he said with his mind. And when Thundar hit the ground, it sounded like thunder. Now, his body seemed to disappear then reappear about ten feet ahead. After that, he continued fading in and out of vision until he had shot past Prince Saka. A post-thunderous rumble resonated heavily through the enormous, underground cavern. As his feet hit with a groundbreaking power, it propelled Thundar to produce an unmistakable sonic boom. "**Now Saka, concentrate and catch me**," said Thundar. And in a few seconds, Saka caused the same booming sound and tackled Thundar. They slammed into the wall and laid on the ground for a while just looking at each other, laughing.

Then Saka said, "I noticed every time I heard the boom, I could feel it even when you were way over there. And after the first boom, every time you changed direction, another one occurred. I wonder what being near you when you boom is like," said Saka.

"Okay, let's see," said Thundar. This time, he caused a boom as soon as he took off. Then another boom, then another! Now making the circle coming towards Saka, he asked him, "**Are you ready, brother?**"

"**Okay then,**" he replied. Boom, boom, boom, Thundar sounded off as he pulsated, bearing down on Saka's position. When he got just inches away from him, he stopped and looked him in the eyes. Both of them smiled and all in a millisecond changed direction and caused a boom louder than any one before. It shot Prince Saka twenty feet in the air. Then when he came down, he let himself roll as far as the force from the boom pushed until he slammed into the wall, but this time he landed on his feet. He was not hurt in the least.

"Oh, Great Yeshua, I feel indestructible," said Saka. "So do I, brother," said Thundar.

"Okay, that's enough for today. I sent some men to retrieve the skeleton of the giant. I am leaving to oversee the transport. I might be a couple of days, so make yourselves at home because this is your home. Wait till you see your new rooms," said the King.

"We have our own rooms?" asked Saka.

"Absolutely, they are identical in every way, with your own toilets, tubs and running water. You are both going to love them."

Chapter XXI

Girl of My Dreams

Weeks passed and Icya stayed alert and laid low. Outside, she was Mykail and, inside her room, she was herself, only going outside to get food and other things she needed. She spent most of her day reading books or writing in her diary, but mostly she read the Dark Grimoires. It was filled with very old and powerful spells and rituals, the majority of which were evil in nature. But a few of them would help her in the very near future.

One night, Icya awoke from a dream that had been reoccurring every night for about a week. She got up, lit a few candles, grabbed her diary and began to write about what happened in her dream. In her diary, she wrote, "Tonight in my dream, I woke up to Saka lying beside me. I could feel his breath on the back of my neck. Then I turned around and he was looking back at me with tears in his eyes. It was so real, like he was really here.

The first night I had this dream, I remember being startled a little by the sight of him, but I guess since the dream is happening over and over again, I have gotten used to it. When I noticed him crying, I got up, grabbed a cloth that was hanging on my clothesline, sat down beside him, and wiped the tears from his eyes while asking him why he was crying, but each night he remained silent. My heart hurt so much to see him cry to the point where I used to wake myself out of the dream from a cold, wet pillow full of my own tears.

One night, Icya awoke from a dream that had been reoccurring every night for about a week. She got up, lit a few candles, grabbed her diary and began to write about what happened in her dream. In her diary, she wrote, "Tonight in my dream, I woke up to Saka lying beside me. I could feel his breath on the back of my neck. Then I turned around and he was looking back at me with tears in his eyes. It was so real, like he was really here.

The first night I had this dream, I remember being startled a little by the sight of him, but I guess since the dream is happening over and over again, I have gotten used to it. When I noticed him crying, I got up, grabbed a cloth that was hanging on my clothesline, sat down beside him, and wiped the tears from his eyes while asking him why he was crying, but each night he remained silent. My heart hurt so much to see him cry to the point where I used to wake myself out of the dream from a cold, wet pillow full of my own tears.

Tonight, I did not wake up. Instead, I pulled him close to me and kissed him. Then we began to kiss and caress each other. Soon we both were entirely naked and, for the first time, I felt what it must feel like to make love. For hours it seemed my body and soul were connected to him in complete, blissful harmony. I truly felt like I was in control of this dream, and this morning I remember telling myself that I wasn't going to wake up crying. I was going to try my best to stay asleep so I could be there for him and comfort him, and that is what I did. If I could have remained asleep and be with him forever, this world would never see the whites of my eyes again.

I can still smell him. He smells so good. Anyway, these reoccurring dreams and a ritual I read about in the Dark Grimoires called Rèv Okipan (translated as Dream Invader) gave me an idea. For weeks now, I have been trying to come up with a way to see him, speak with him, return the Dark Grimoires, and convince him that I had nothing to do with what happened at the celebration. I cannot go to him directly because he is most likely upset with me and will have me arrested before I can explain myself. I have to find some other way, and I believe the ritual that I have come across is dangerous, but it is the safest way to speak with him.

This ritual Rèv Okipan requires me to obtain at least one strand of Saka's hair. That is the one ingredient that I do not have. The rest I have gone out and bought from nearby merchants. If done correctly, I will be able to appear in his dreams and speak to him for a very brief moment, by way of my soul leaving my body and going to him in his sleep. The only thing that scares me is that if I do this incorrectly and something disturbs me while I am in the trance, my soul will be in his dreams, leaving my body lifeless forever. I would have to perform this ritual several times because the effects of the ritual don't last long.

After I have explained to him what has been going on and let him know about the evil things my father has been up to, maybe I can go to him myself. I have to find a way to get some hair from him." After Icya put away her diary and blew out the candles, she fell back onto her bed and drifted off into a deep sleep.

The next morning, she got up bright and early with a stressed look on her face. For about thirty minutes, she stared out of her window in deep thought. While looking out of the window, a bird swooping down to snatch some bread crumbs interrupted her train of thought. She watched the bird for a little while, then turned around, got the cloth that hung from a clothesline across her room and stared at it for a minute. She then bathed herself, got dressed, said a quick prayer, opened the window, turned into the bird and flew outside.

Flying over the city gave her an altogether new aspect of the city. It was incredible. There were buildings made almost completely of glass and crystal. These buildings were almost impossible to look at directly in the daytime. The army was massive. There were soldiers in groups all over the city in tight formations. Everyone was in uniform, even the children.

For hours, she hovered, then rested, hoping to see Saka, until at last she came upon a large crowd of people standing in front of the central building. Zolatar and Volaris were in the middle of the crowd. She hovered overhead for a while. Then she saw Saka and Thundar coming out of that building, both dressed in blue, black and gold armor with red turbans on their heads. There were about six guards, three in the front and three in the back. Saka and his brother were finishing training for the day and were on their way to Hazina Palace. Dozens of people followed behind them as they went on their way, sitting high atop the two master rhino and riding along. At first, both of the brothers went fairly slowly but, after a while, they picked up the pace and left the crowd behind. Icya the bird stayed behind the cloak of buildings and trees so that the boys would not notice her following them.

It was dark now, and they were approaching the palace. The boys and the guards slowed down and continued in a slow gallop, while Icya remained in the cloak of the trees close by. High above the ground, Icya could things that no one on the ground could see: soldiers hidden in the tops of the trees, in small treehouses, connected together by bridges. Some of the houses were big enough for one person to fit in, but others were big enough to accommodate ten or more.

Everything was going okay until they came upon a place where there were no trees. The guards were gone also, and a soft, radiating light lit up the treeless grassy forest floor like the sun in the late afternoon. Icya swiftly turned to the right so that she might find some cover of trees, but soon realized that there were no trees for acres that way, in front of her or to the left. Her only choice would be to fly higher, so she did.

Now for the first time, she could see Hazina Palace, and what a sight to behold. It was by far the biggest, tallest, most beautiful castle she had ever seen. This colossal palace -- built upon the base of hundreds of enormous tree stumps that all stood at least twenty feet high on both sides and ten feet high in the centerpiece -- gave a new meaning to the word treehouse. The closer they got to the palace, the brighter it got. There were very tall, wooden beams with torches at the top of them shining light onto the field, and that light was reflecting off the huge gold and crystal palace door.

All of a sudden with no hesitation, Icya swooped down, grabbed Saka's turban and flew like the wind towards the castle. Saka yelled, "Hey, give me that back," but he was helpless because he was not wearing the amulet and she was so fast. Icya eventually made her way back to her room and changed back into herself. She searched the turban for some strands of Saka's hair and, luckily, she found one. After putting the hair strand in a safe place, she retired for the night.

A couple of days passed. Saka and Thundar had made it home from training. Fatigued from a rigorous workout, they both retired to their rooms and went straight to sleep. In the middle of the night, Saka became restless, tossing and turning in his sleep until he woke up and saw Thundar standing in his doorway.

Walking over to Saka's bedside, he signed, "What's wrong, can't sleep?"

"You too, huh," replied Saka as he sat up and wiped his eyes clean of crust.

"I've been having a reoccurring dream that becomes longer and more vivid every night," said Saka.

"Tell me about these dreams," said Thundar as he sat down on the floor beside the bed.

"Well, that girl Princess Icya is in all of them. In the beginning of the dreams, we are all at our last birthday celebration. Things are going just as they went that day, until all of a sudden you start sneezing uncontrollably and walk off to yourself. Then when I turn my head back towards the audience, there is no one there. Everyone is gone except Princess Icya, and she is standing right behind me whispering in my ear. I try to move to look at her, but I can't move," said Saka.

"What did she say?" signed Thundar.

"She said that we were in grave danger, and it was her father who was to blame for what happened at the celebration. I can still smell her perfume. Then, when I am finally able to turn around, I look in her eyes. I become frozen again. She then puts her arms around me, stares at me for two or three minutes, then kisses me and disappears like mist into the air.

After she disappears, I'm able to move again, but then everything changes and I end up in the field fighting off a flock of birds. It is very strange. When I look into her eyes, it is like I knew her," said Saka with a confused look on his face.

"I don't know what to think about that dream. Everyone is sure she was to blame. She did show up at the celebration in Congion's carriage and changed into a bird and flew off right before the dead people came," signed Thundar as he stood up.

"Wait a minute. That is right. Father did say he believed she changed into a bird and flew away. What kind of bird did he say it was?" asked Saka.

"A peregrine falcon," both of them said at the same time while looking at each other.

"The same bird from the other night! Okay then, we need to tell Father tomorrow," said Saka.

"Okay, goodnight," signed Thundar.

"Goodnight, brother," replied Saka. Thundar went to his room, and both of them went to sleep.

A couple of weeks went by and Saka had not had any more dreams about Icya. With all the extensive training and adventuring in this strange, new kingdom that King O'Saka had built, Saka forgot to tell his father about his dreams.

For the next six months, the brothers trained and perfected the link. Quickly, they learned from their father's book and from the generals how to fight as one. They realized that physically, Thundar would always be stronger than Saka but mentally Saka could achieve a lot more than his brother could. Only the fact that Thundar had been exposed to the talisman years before Saka kept the learning on the same pace.

One morning, Saka arose unusually early, got dressed and went to find his father. When Saka found him, King O'Saka was sitting in a beautifully made snakeskin and ivory chaise lounge, smoking on his pipe while playing his long-neck guitar. "Good morning, Father," said Saka.

"Good morning, son. How are you?" he asked.

"I'm okay, but I've been having some strange dreams about Princess Icya," said Saka.

"Um, the young lady from the last celebration," the King said as he put his guitar down beside him and sat up straight to give Saka his full attention. "Well, son, you're at the age now when young men have desires that need to be met one way or the other," said King O'Saka before Saka interrupted him and said, "No, Dad, not like that. Okay then," said Saka, looking to the side and slightly embarrassed.

"Oh, okay, well tell me about it," said King O'Saka. Saka went on to tell him about the first couple of dreams. Then he told his father that in his dreams, Icya told him that somehow her father, Congion, has been controlling and getting information about what goes on in the kingdom from Elder Sheshon and that if I don't believe her to tell Elder Sheshon that His daughter Nettie was murdered about seven months ago and watch his reaction. Saka also told King O'Saka that Icya had something in her possession that belonged to him and, in his dream, she said she wanted to give it back.

After Saka finished giving his father a review of his weird dreams, the king sat back in his chair, took it all in for a moment, then sat up and said, " I told you this girl transformed into a bird and flew away. Now you tell me that the same kind of bird stole your turban off your head, and you are having abnormally vivid dreams about this girl and the bird. Okay then, she is using black magic to contact you through your dreams. Did she say when she wanted to return the item she claims belongs to me?" asked the King.

"No, Father, but she did say she would only give it back if we could forgive her for taking it in the first place," replied Saka.

"I see, well in the meantime, we will see what Elder Sheshon has to say about her allegations. His daughter disappeared around the same time that Congion and his group went missing. Maybe Congion has been speaking to Sheshon in his dreams, controlling him with promises of reuniting with Nettie and threats of killing her if he does not do as he commanded. We will see."

Chapter XXII

Night Terror

Back in Ardhi Anasa, Zulin was missing Saka badly. They wrote back and forth almost every week. They had not seen each other for months and her birthday was coming up, so she decided to go to Hazina to surprise Saka. Even though in the letters that Saka had written, he told her not to travel through the forest because of stories that were spreading about a flying monster, she was very excited about the idea of seeing Saka and also very eager to see how the amulets' power had changed him. She could hardly wait, and nothing would turn her from going to see him.

Five days before her birthday, Zulin and Cedona, a personal servant, left for Hazina in a mid-size carriage surrounded by ten guards on horseback. Saka had no idea that she was coming. On the way there, Zulin and Cedona talked like two schoolgirls on their first date.

"I can't wait to see him. The way he described Hazina is like paradise in a dream," said Zulin with absolute glee in her eyes.

"Yeah, especially since he's there," said Cedona, laughing a little.

"Okay, laugh all you want. I'm going to hook you up with Thundar! Hahahaha," laughed Zulin.

"Eww! You cannot be serious!" replied Cedona.

"Stop playing. You know you like the dark, mysterious, silent type. Ha, you know you love brother," Zulin said jokingly while spraying some perfume on her neck.

"Please stop playing like that! You are so crazy! Brother better go sit his butt down somewhere," said Cedona, laughing a little. "That really smells good, Zulin. Can I put a little on me?" asked Cedona.

"Here you go," replied Zulin, handing her the bottle of perfume.

Zulin and Cedona had been talking and laughing for hours until they stopped to set up camp for the night. The guards had lit fires and started cooking. It was nice and quiet. "Hey, Cedona, look who it is," said Zulin, smiling a little.

"Who is it?" asked Cedona, looking around. "Cedona," said Kintu (newly promoted commander of the guards) as he walked towards their carriage.

"Oh, hello Kintu, lovely night isn't it," said Cedona, flirting a little.

"Yeah, it is, but the horses are a bit spooked for some reason," said Commander Kintu.

"Ahh, it will be fine. You know how those animals are, frightened over nothing. Anyway, what are you doing? Is that a new uniform?" inquired Cedona.

"No, but that's some new perfume you have on, isn't it?" he replied.

"Yes. Do you like it?" she asked.

"Nah, I'm not really a perfume man," he replied, laughing a little.

"Really," said Cedona.

"I'm just playing, Cedona. You smell really good," he replied. They both went out behind the carriage and continued to talk.

Meanwhile, back at Hazina, Saka and Thundar were at the diamond cavern, training with Master Yasufe. This would mark the last day of training for the boys. In the past six months, the princes had learned a lifetime's worth of training and were able to execute their combative moves with the precision of someone with a hundred years' experience. Master Yasufe and General Nakatu swore they were the best the world has ever seen.

At the end of training, a small ceremony was held for Saka and his brother in honor of their accomplishments. Together, King O'Saka and Master Yasufe had forged the princes some very special weapons. For Prince Saka, they forged an oversized, indestructible, golden-tipped sword with a blue handle.

For Thundar, they made a super-sized javelin of the colors, with two retractable, curved diamond-tipped spikes, also indestructible. Both of them also received blades identical to the one Zulin received from Master Yasufe.

Finally, yet importantly, they received new warrior armor made of the same indestructible metal. Prince Saka and Prince Thundar received these honors and gifts with great pride. And after the gifts were given, the Grand Elder, who was under the impression that he had traveled from Ardhi Anasa just for the ceremony, prayed a prayer to Yeshua to watch over them and help them lead their people through this new world that he had made for them.

After the ceremony, King O'Saka asked Elder Sheshon to stay and talk for a bit while everyone else retired to their rooms for the night. Elder Sheshon was a short, very dark- skinned, bug-eyed seventy-year-old man. He had a long, gray beard that nearly touched the ground.

"How was your journey, Sheshon?" asked King O'Saka. "My King, it was long and hot but worth every bead of sweat to Be here for this great ceremony. Saka and Thundar are marvels Of the world, and the city that you have built for them will be known as the center of the world, but O'Saka what in God's name is that dead giant doing at the gates of Hazina? That was the scariest thing that I have ever encountered in my life," said Elder Sheshon.

"Scarier than the thought of your long-lost daughter dying in the hand of a murderous voodoo king?" replied King O'Saka as he watched Sheshon's body language.

Sheshon stood there for a few seconds with a confused look on his face. Then he straightened his face and said," No, sire, I can think of no scarier thought than that."

"Okay then! What about the thought of you being executed for endangering the lives of everyone, including my sons and I. Treason, how does that make you feel, Sheshon?"

King O'Saka asked sternly, looking Elder Sheshon square in the eyes. For a minute, the elder tried to keep a straight face and keep looking back into the eyes of the King, but soon tears started to fall.

"Oh my King, please forgive me. Congion came to me in my dreams with my daughter Nettie. She was years older than when he took her. In my dreams, I did not give a second thought when he threatened to kill her in front of me. I would have never betrayed you, O'Saka. I know I should have come to you, but he has my daughter and if a man can come into your dreams anytime he feels like it, there is no telling what other horrible magic he can perform," said Elder Sheshon, drowning in his own tears.

"Well, if the person who revealed to me your treachery is truthful indeed, then your daughter may already be dead! You should have come to me, Sheshon. We could have put our heads together and come up with something," yelled the King.

"I am your dear friend. Do not persecute me for things I had the least control of. Please, my King! I did not believe it was real half of the time. He was in my dreams, my King," said Sheshon, down on his knees and pleading his case.

"Guards, confine him to his room until I decide what to do with him."

Later that night, Saka awoke to his father's voice.

"Dreaming, my son?" he said. "Luckily, no, Father," replied Saka as he sat up and wiped his eyes. " So I talked to Elder Sheshon last night. He confirmed what was revealed to you in your dreams. He betrayed us and has put both Hazina and Ardhi Anasa in a bit of a quagmire. For years, he has been telling that snake Congion everything he wants to know. Everything that I told him in confidence, he told Congion in secret. I think I will call on the council of an old friend. The great voodoo king Pouvwa Bondye is a wise and powerful man. He will be the best resource in this matter of dreams and magic. He was Congion's mentor," said King O'Saka.

"So in the meantime, should me and brother try to find Icya to see what it is she claims is yours?" asked Saka, getting out of his bed.

"No, son, we have hundreds of thousands of men for that sort of thing! I'll get right on it," said King O'Saka.

"But, Father, I was thinking it would be easier if I met up with her like she suggested in my dreams. If provoked, she could easily slip through the hands of the men or worse spook them enough to kill her," said Saka.

"Okay then. Let's do it your way, but be careful, Saka. This girl of your dreams is also the daughter of our enemy and by any standard makes her our enemy until proven otherwise," said the King.

"Okay, Father," replied Saka.

"Well, sweet dreams. I'll see you guys in the morning," said King O'Saka as he left the room.

Back inside the carriage, Zulin was just relaxing, looking at a pocket-sized drawing of Saka and humming a song her mom used to hum to her when she was a baby. "I'm coming, my love," Zulin whispered to herself.

Meanwhile, one of the men went to scout around the perimeter. He had made it about a hundred feet in front of them when he heard something in the distance that sounded like a woman's scream, but not exactly. "Hello! Is anybody out there?" yelled the guard. Then the guard heard the same sound again, but this time it was closer. "Who's there? Show yourself," yelled the guard, a tad bit frightened. The guard stopped his horse, lifted his torch high and looked in all directions.

"Fanm menm bagay la tou moun, Popobawa," said the monster with a hideous voice that screeched and rumbled. The awful voice seemed to have two or more octaves.

"Come out, you idiot. Popobawa is not real. It's a tale told to children to keep them from roaming the forest alone at night. Stop playing around before something bad happens to you out here," the guard yelled nervously.

"Soooo, do your eyes deceive you?" asked the hideous voice as it now presented itself in front of the guard. The legend of Popobawa was as real as the terror in his eyes. The enormous ten-foot, bat-winged, one-eyed monster flapped his wings and hovered directly in the path of the guard. Its wings were so powerful that the wind from them pushed the horse to the ground, crushing the left leg of the guard.

"Arrrrh!" the guard yelled in pain. Commander Kintu heard the commotion, kissed Cedona on the cheek, and told her to go inside the carriage. He and some other guards then raced over to where the guard was. Oh my God, you're real," whispered the hurt guard to himself, picking up the torch and looking around to find the quickest way to escape.

"Commander Kintu!" he screamed.

"Come with meeee," said the horrifying creature as he swooped up the guard and flew straight up off into the dark night sky, leaving one of his legs still under the horse.. A minute later, Commander Kintu and the others showed up, and the torch came hurling down out of the sky, almost hitting one of the men. They could hear the guard screaming until he was either too far to hear, or dead.

"Addo! Addo!" yelled Commander Kintu as he unknowingly stood in a puddle of blood.

"Sir, look down at your feet," said one of the men.

"Oh my goodness, what happened to this horse?" asked Commander Kintu.

"The blood is not from the horse, sir. Addo's leg is under it," said the guard.

"Awww man. Addo!" yelled the commander.

Back in Zulin's carriage, Zulin and Cedona were wondering what was going on. Cedona stepped outside, put her hands on her hips and yelled, "Commander Kintu, what is it?"

"Get back in your carriage," yelled the commander.

As soon as he said that, everyone could hear something flapping in the wind and coming down through the trees. Cedona looked up and could see something falling. Then splat, Addo's dead body hit the ground, and the blood went in Cedona's eyes. She screamed and ran back inside the carriage. Now as the men ran back towards Zulin's carriage, they could hear the loud flapping of the monster's wings and its horrible screeching voice saying something in a foreign tongue. Then out of the trees, it swiftly approached, flying directly at a group of the guards with its wings spread wide.

Three guards got ready to strike, but when they swung their swords, the one-eyed beast has already passed to the other side of them and cut their bodies in half. "The rest of you, defend the carriage with your last breath," commanded Kintu, in fighting position by the door of the carriage.

Inside the carriage, Cedona was having a hard time keeping Zulin from going outside to fight.

"No, Zulin. Whatever is out there, it's not human. He said to stay in here!" demanded Cedona.

"But what is that thing? Why is it after us?" said Zulin, frightened but ready to go outside and fight for her life.

"Please be quiet, Zulin, so we can hear what's going on. "Who are you? What do you want with us, demon?" demanded Commander Kintu. "Popobawa, do you know of me?" asked the creature.

"Popobawa, yes, I've heard tales of an evil monster that rapes men and woman before he kills them," said the commander.

"Well, do you believe?" asked the monster, sounding as if it was getting closer and closer to the carriage.

"No, and I don't believe you're getting any of this tonight, whatever your name is. Kill him," yelled Commander Kintu. For a very short period of time, Zulin and Cedona could hear the men yelling and trying to fight the monster, but soon those yells turned to screams of great pain and death. Then there was silence.

"Why is it so quiet out there all of a sudden?" whispered

Cedona, crying and shaking franticly.

"I don't know, Cedona. Do you think they're dead? What is that smell?" whispered Zulin.

"What are you going to do?" asked Cedona.

"Just be quiet," whispered Zulin, grabbing her sword.

Meanwhile, outside was an all-out bloodbath, with body parts everywhere. Commander Kintu was the only man left alive. He was bleeding badly and unconscious. Popobawa was dragging him by both legs with one hand getting ready to fly away with him until the monster stopped and started sniffing the air. At first, it was turned away from the carriage. Now, it was sniffing and walking towards the carriage. Slowly coming to, Commander Kintu saw it sniffing and realized that it must have caught a whiff of the perfume and is going to find Zulin and Cedona if he doesn't do something.

"Hey, you stinking, one-eyed fool! What happened to our night on the town?" screamed the badly wounded commander as he pulled a dagger from his boot in a failed attempt to stab the monster. The creature just looked at him, sniffed the air again, glanced at the carriage and then slung the commander so far into the trees that he could not be seen. Now, its full attention was on Zulin's carriage.

"Ahhh, how I loathe the smell of magnolia, but when mixed with a hint of lily flowers, it arouses the senses," the hideous beast said while ravenously licking the door of the carriage.

"Get behind me, Cedona," whispered Zulin as she gripped her sword and backed away from the door. Looking through small cracks in the carriage, Zulin saw the beast circling them. She drew her sword back and waited patiently for it to get closer to a larger hole while a terrified Cedona whimpered behind her. "Shut up, Cedona," whispered Zulin as she concentrated on the monster's position. Then as soon as Popobawa looked inside the crack, she thrust the sword through the hole directly into its eye socket. "Arrrrh," it screamed as Zulin attempted to pull the sword from its head.

The monster then grabbed the sword and with its other hand punched the carriage with so much force that it knocked the entire carriage off its wheels and sent Zulin and Cedona through the other side, crashing to the ground. The monster screamed in agony while it tried to pull the sword out of its eye, not noticing that the two young ladies were out in the open.

Zulin eventually woke up from being briefly unconscious and saw a sword on the ground next to her. She woke up Cedona and told her to run. "What are you doing? Come with me, Zulin," said Cedona.

"No! Run, Cedona. He'll kill both of us," replied Zulin as she pushed Cedona with her foot. "Go! Here he comes," said Zulin as she watched the monster pull the sword from its eye socket and at the same time watching Cedona run deep into the woods.

"Arrrrh," screamed the enraged monster as it ran towards Zulin. "Come on, stinky! After I kill you, I'm going to drag your butt to the river and throw you in so nobody else has to smell you," said Zulin, gritting her teeth with both hands on the sword, ready to defend herself.

The monster slashed with its right and then with its left. Zulin dodged both attempts. The beast then tried to kick Zulin, but she blocked it with her sword. The blocked blow sent her tumbling ten feet through some bushes. Now Popobawa had lost sight of her, but he could still smell the perfume she was wearing. He slashed through the bushes, searching and getting closer to Zulin, so she eased herself behind a big tree.

He got closer to the tree, so she moved around the tree. Seeing a chance for a clean strike, she took it. "Arrrrh," she screamed as she swung the sword with all her might and struck it in the back of the neck, but the sword did no damage at all. The beast just turned around, looked at Zulin and smiled. "Oh it's like that, huh, butt breath," said Zulin as she slashed at the beast, missing when it jumped in the air, flapped its wings twice, and rose about twenty feet above Zulin. The force of the wind caused her to collapse to her knees. Then the monster came down fast and punched Zulin so hard she went two feet into the ground. It then grabbed unconscious Zulin by her waist and took off in the air.

Hundreds of feet in the clouds, dangling in the powerful grasp of this hideous, murderous, one-eyed monster, Zulin opened her eyes. Having a pretty good idea that the rest of the night was going to be downhill from here, she reached in the side of her brassiere, pulled out the diamond-tipped blade that her dad had given her, and sliced off three of the monster's fingers. It let her go, screaming in agony, and while she plummeted downward, she pulled out the picture of Saka, put it over her heart, smiled and began singing the song her mom used to sing to her. Then she fell to her unavoidable and untimely death.

Meanwhile, on the run deep in the forest, Cedona moved quickly, trying to find her way back home through the darkness. With only the light of a crescent moon peeking through the thick foliage of the trees, Cedona was scared, alone and extensively lost. While she ran frantically in an unknown direction, she heard something rustling in the bushes slightly ahead of her, so she stopped and ducked down.

"Help me! Is someone there?" mumbled a voice from the bushes about ten feet ahead of her. Cedona stayed down, completely flat on the forest floor, breathing heavily but trying not to be heard. "Who is that? I know you are there. I can hear you breathing. Please help me," said the voice in the bushes. Cedona picked up her head and said, "Kintu, is that you?"

"Yes! Who is that? Is that Cedona?" asked Kintu, barely alive.

"Yes, it's me. Where are you?" asked Cedona as she stood up and looked around for him.

"I'm over here," said Kintu as he put up his hand and shook the bushes where he lay in a puddle of his blood. Cedona ran over to him, sat down and pulled him onto her lap.

"Oh my God! You're hurt bad, Kintu," said Cedona, as She pressed her hand down in his stomach, trying to slow the bleeding coming from a large, gaping cut.

"I know. Where is Zulin?" he asked, gasping for breath.

"I do not know. She made me run. I begged her to come with me. She would not listen. She stayed there. She was fighting that monster! Oh God, Zulin," whispered Cedona as she cried and looked into the night sky. Her tears fell onto Kintu's face as she wept.

"Don't cry. I need you to be strong for the both of us," said Kintu in great pain as his bottom lip trembled.

"Listen, Cedona, we need to make it back to the palace and tell the others, and I won't make it unless you stop crying and help me," he said, looking directly up into Cedona's water-filled eyes. After a minute or two, Cedona stopped crying, and Kintu instructed her to rip off the bottom of her dress so she could wrap the wound on his chest. After she wrapped the wound, he told her to help him stand up. He was in too bad of shape to stand on his own, and by no means could he walk all the way back to the palace, even with her help.

"How are we going to get home when you can barely even stand? I cannot carry you," said Cedona, starting to cry again.

"Calm down, my sweet flower, we have a ride," said Kintu, holding on firmly to Cedona's shoulders. Then he sounded out a short, piercing whistle. Out of the shadows appeared a big, black, beautiful horse. It scared Cedona. She almost screamed. "Hey, boy, thank you for waiting for me," said Kintu as he rubbed his horse's head. "Help me get on," he said to Cedona. Both of them got on the horse and traveled all night, and part of the day, until they reached the palace.

Chapter XXIII

Oh Great Yeshua

Back in Hazina, Saka and Thundar are unaware of the horrible and tragic events that had transpired deep in the woods and were busy executing a plan to find Icya.

The first part of the plan would be to let her know that they were looking for her and that she won't be arrested on sight. Saka thought that the easiest way to do that would be to make an announcement that everyone could hear but wouldn't understand. So they put on the amulets and went behind the castle. Then Saka jumped high in the sky, rising and rising. He had gotten to at least one hundred feet in the air and still rising. Then with his super voice, he said, "To the daughter of our enemy, we need not be enemies anymore,for what you have spoken is proven to be true. Come to me inour frequent meeting place and tell me where you would liketo meet!" His voice could be heard clearly from dozens ofmiles away. After the aerial announcement, he started to comedown very hard and fast, making a whistling sound, but when he hit the ground, there was almost no sound or sign of impact, just a little dust. Instead, he slid his right leg to the right towards a very large tree and, in a millisecond, booooom, that tree exploded into thousands of pieces, leaving a hole the size of three elephants.

"Ohhhhhhhh!" exclaimed both of the boys. "That was crazy, bruh! I hope she knows it was me. I bet the people around the city thought it was God himself talking. Hahaha! Somebody is under their bed right now," said Prince Saka, laughing while Thundar shook his head yes and chuckled a little.

"Come on, brother, I'm hungry. Let's go get some breakfast," said Thundar.

The boys ate breakfast and went about their day as usual. That night, while Saka and Thundar lay asleep in their beds, one of the guards from Ardhi Anasa arrived and reported to the King the events that took place in the woods with Zulin. He also reported that they had found Zulin's body in the Karura Forest, not too far from where everything had taken place, and the only two survivors were back in Ardhi Anasa safe and sound.

When the King heard this terrifying news, he slowly closed his eyes and very calmly said, "And who is responsible for this?" The guard told him what Commander Kintu and Cedona had told him.

At first, he looked at the guard in disbelief and asked the guard, "Did Commander Kintu tell you this with a clear mind?"

"Yes, sire, he was barely alive, but his mind was sound and the servant Cedona confirmed every word. There are men everywhere looking for the beast now in the Karura Forest," replied the guard.

"Good, find it, kill it and bring it to me! Go, and say nothing of this to anyone in the city. I need time to figure out how I will give this terrible news to Prince Saka and her father," said the King. King O'Saka then turned around and began to walk away with tears forming in his eyes. At first, the King did not know what or how to say what needed to be said, so he went to his room, got down on his knees and began to pray.

"Oh great Yeshua, please help me, Lord. I have been a loyal and obedient servant. You have blessed me with riches and worldly possessions that cannot be summed up in any conceivable amount. But my most precious gift, my son, oh Mighty Father, is about to receive a blow to his heart and soul to which many mighty men have never recovered. Oh God, give me the knowledge to say the right words, oh Lord, to be the father and friend that my family needs right now in the most troublesome of times. Tell me, what should I do? What should I say? In your name I pray. Amen.

For about thirty minutes, he remained beside his bed on his knees with his hands together and his head down. Then he calmly stood up, walked out of his room down the long hallway towards Saka's room but passed it up and went into Thundar's room instead. He opened the door, walked over to the bed where Thundar lay fast asleep and gently tapped him on the shoulder.

Thundar opened his eyes and realized that something was not right with the King. "Father, what's wrong? Is Saka alright?" asked Thundar in sign. "He is fine, but his beloved Zulin has been murdered," replied the King. Thundar just stared at King O'Saka for a while, then his cheeks began to puff out and deflate rapidly. "Calm down, son, I need you to be calm for your brother's sake because I've thought about it and I know what the undeniable outcome will be after we tell him about the tragedy. He will kill whoever took her life, and I will help him," said the King, now standing by a chest where Thundar kept his medallion. "Who did it, Father?" signed Thundar. "Wait, my son. The men say it was a beast that called itself Popobawa, a very powerful, magical beast of ancient times. Promise me you will let no harm come to Saka, and you will fight as one like you have been taught Promise me!" yelled the King as he grabbed the medallion from Thundar's hand.

"I promise, Father," signed Thundar.

"I could not stand to lose either of you. It would kill me. I would not have a reason to live. Okay, first we have to find out if the girl Icya had spoken to him in his dreams. That way, I can go to meet her to try to find out where her father is. He is to blame for all of this. While you and Saka go to kill this Popobawa, I will prepare the army and we will find Congion and rid this planet of his infectious evil once and for all," pronounced the King as he gave Thundar his amulet back.

When they got to Saka's room, he was already awake and sitting up on the side of his bed with a candle lit. "Father, what's wrong?" asked the Prince with a very concerned look on his face.

"Son, I need to know if the girl Icya has come to you in your sleep tonight," said the King.

"Oh, yes, she did. Princess Icya said she wanted to meet alone in front of my statue when the sun goes down later tonight," said Saka, looking up at Thundar and wondering why his best friend had not looked him in the eyes since he walked into the room.

"Okay, that's good," replied King O'Saka.

"Brother, what's wrong?" asked Saka. Thundar looked at him with pure despair, then he turned his eyes to King O'Saka, awaiting his words.

"Son, I have something to tell you and I really need you to be strong. Promise me you'll be strong, son," said King

O'Saka as he got down on one knee in front of the Prince. "Okay, Father, what's going on?" replied Saka.

"A little while ago, one of the soldiers from Ardhi Anasa came to report that on the way to come to see you, Zulin was murdered deep in the Karura Forest. She was going to surprise you," said King O'Saka, holding both of Saka's hands.

"What … no … that's not true … that's not … my Zulin? You're talking about my Zulin?" asked Saka as he looked to Thundar.

Thundar looked at him and signed, "She's gone, brother" and slowly put down his hands.

"Noooooo, but how, who, I want to see her. Where is she?" yelled Saka as he got up and started to get dressed, then fell back down on the side of his bed.

"Her body is in Ardhi Anasa," said the King as he sat beside Saka and put his arms around him. tears.

"Who did it, Father?" asked Saka with a face full of

"Commander Kintu claims that a one-eyed, winged beast called Popobawa is responsible for this," said the King.

"What, what are you saying? That she was killed by the Popobawa of myth? What was done to her? How did she die?" asked Saka with apparent rage building up.

"She was beaten very badly and her neck and back were broken," replied the King, looking down toward the ground.

"Ahrrrrrhr," screamed Prince Saka as King O'Saka and Thundar grabbed him and held him.

"I know, son. I'm sorry, Saka! Oh, I love you so much, Saka," said King O'Saka as he held him and rubbed his back. For about ten minutes, Saka wept in his brother and father's arms, then he stopped crying and said, "First, I must go see her, and then I will kill this Popobawa!"

Meanwhile, high in the sky above the front gates of Hazina, Popobawa subsequently came across Icya's scent. He brought Legion along with him.

Carrying him in his talons, too high for anyone to see in the night sky, Popobawa let go of Legion and began to descend rapidly towards the giant corpse of the Nephlim. Legion was so high in the sky that it took at least five minutes before boooom, he hit the ground right on side of the Nephlim and went under the surface about ten feet deep. He unburied himself and, with superhuman speed, he ran to the head of the dead giant and placed his hands upon its head.

Chapter XXIV

Enemy at the Gates, Death From Above

Back in Saka's room, the three of them stood up from the bed, and the boys looked at each other, clinching their teeth with anger. "Go, my sons, and do what you must. I will go meet the young lady," said the King, now looking at Saka with a confused look in his eyes.

"You feel that?" asked Saka.

"Yeah, what is that?" asked King O'Saka as the ground beneath their feet went from a small, vibrating sound to a thunderous rumbling. "Come on, let's go see what the hell is going on out there," he said as they ran towards the palace doors, stumbling through the long hallway.

As they reached the large crystal doors, neither one of them could believe what they saw. The once-deceased giant Nephlim skeleton that lay in front of the palace gates was now standing over the trees, belting out a deep, long, vibrating yell.

"Oh, my Lord," said King O'Saka as he looked up to the sky at the monstrous, ancient giant.

"That's it!" yelled Saka as he and Thundar put their amulets around their necks and transformed. Now radiating with the power of the amulets, Thundar looked at Saka and said," Okay then! Then boom, boom, the boys blasted off towards the Nephlim, but the force from the supersonic boom lifted King O'Saka ten feet off the ground. Luckily, Thundar noticed what had happened, so he zoomed back, caught the King before he hit the ground, sat him down gently and jogged about twenty feet away from the King, then boom, he was gone, and, in a flash, he caught up with Saka.

Now coming upon the trees in front of the castle, they both jumped one hundred feet in the air and then Thundar said with his super voice, "Sound the alarm, battalions twenty through fifty, formulate your squadrons between the forest camp and the castle. All the remaining battalions report to the front gates, ready for battle. Women and children get as far away from the front gates as possible. Go to the castle now. This is not a drill. I repeat, this is not a drill!"

Still rising higher and advancing towards the position of the Nephlim, Saka and Thundar could see that the giant had crossed over the city gates and was now destroying the city. It had already killed dozens of people, and large numbers were trapped under the rubble. The army presence fighting the Nephlim was having no effect on it whatsoever. "All battalions near the giant, back away from it," commanded Thundar. Then, with no hesitation, he pulled his sphere from its holster and threw it thousands of feet, penetrating through the giant's head. The effect was that of a mosquito bite. The people screamed as he stumped and crushed buildings with his enormous fist.

When Saka and Thundar initially came down, they were in the middle of the city. They took off again. This time, there were three consecutive booms. They were moving so fast that their bodies were invisible. When they did become visible, they were high in the sky over the giant, coming down hard and fast on each side of him. As they came down on the side of the giant's head, Saka and Thundar screamed with all their might into the Nephlim's ears. His earholes were as big as Saka and Thundar put together, and the force from their super voices rocked the giant, causing him to stumble backwards. Then right before the boys simultaneously hit the ground, Saka yelled out, "Impact direction spiral uppercut!"

As soon as they both hit the ground, making almost no sound at all, they slid the foot that was closest to the giant towards him, which caused an explosion that made a huge hole under the Nephlim's feet. He began to stumble and almost fell to one knee. Then the boys burst into the air, delivering a crashing double uppercut to its chin, standing the giant perfectly back up straight. Thundar scraped and clawed his way up to the Nephlim's mouth and grabbed ahold of his rotten, razor-sharp teeth. While Saka descended to the ground below, the giant saw him, raised its hand high over its head, then came down with a ferocious slap that sent Saka hurtling to the ground like a fly being caught by a perfect swat. This swatting produced more downward speed and velocity than Saka or Thundar had ever encountered, so Saka used it against the beast.

"Open his mouth wide, brother. I'm going in!" **said** Saka.

"Okay then," replied Thundar as he wrestled the Nephlim's mouth open, getting beat by the giant. Again, when Saka hit the ground, there was hardly any sound, but this time he came down in a squatting position with his arms bent upwards and spread apart. Then he slowly closed his arms and legs and disappeared. When he reappeared, he was in the mouth, then bursting through the top of the Nephlim's skull and as soon as he was out, Thundar went in. Then Saka came down on top of the giant's cracked head, crawled back inside with his brother and, boom, the Nephlim's head exploded as both yelled and dropkicked both sides of the head.

Saka and Thundar could see the demons exiting from where the head used to be and go down into the body. The giant then started swinging wildly, throwing punches into the air and smashing its fist upon the buildings below. In the midst of its blind rage, it smashed its fist down on the diamond- and ruby-decorated roof of the training center.   "Oh no, not our training facilities," said Thundar as both of them jumped down off the brute.

"We are going to have to break its body down entirely," said Thundar, looking in Saka's direction unaware that the Giant Nephlim had thrown a wild punch coming straight for him. Baalachkum! The punch sent Thundar flying some miles through the air, landing on the front lawn of the palace. Saka saw his brother flying helplessly through the air and lost it. With precision and lightning speed, he ran and punched the right anklebone, then the left one and they shattered like glass. The giant fell to the ground, demolishing everything caught up under it.

Then in a booming blast, he took off towards the castle and jumped high in the sky to see if he could spot Thundar. But before he could find him, Saka saw something flying fast about to enter the woods that led to the wood camp. Still keeping his eye on what he now recognized to be Popobawa, the murderer of his one and only true love, he called to Thundar telepathically, but there was no answer.

Thundar lay in the field, unconscious, bleeding profusely and shimmering with the small and large chunks of diamonds and rubies that were embedded all over his body after the Nephlim megapunched him with its jewel-covered knuckles.

By now, Saka had started to descend but still had not taken his eyes off Popobawa. He turned his body around to make sure he would not lose the flying demon.

Now, as he came down fast out of the sky backwards, he yelled, "Brotheeeerrrrrrr!" The skull- cracking sound woke Thundar up from being knocked out. Popobawa heard the loud noise also and, when Saka looked above him in the sky, he saw a disturbing, deranged stare and bared teeth looking back at him. **"I'm okay, Saka. Diamonds, we are vulnerable to diamonds,"** said Thundar as he struggled to get up and shake the diamond particles from his body.

Chapter XXV

Death of the Funk Era

"Okay, brother. I see what killed Zulin. I'm looking directly at it right now. Go find Father and then go and finish the headless giant," said Saka with pure rage and murder in his voice and on his face.

"I can see Father now. Go crush him into oblivion, brother," replied Thundar as he looked over his shoulder and saw his father and Icya on top of Zolatar, leading half of the army around the castle heading to the back forest. Boom! Thundar took off towards the castle.

Up in the air, Saka was still at the mercy of his descent, so without thinking he started moving his legs back and forth as if he was running. Faster and faster they went until they disappeared, then he tilted over to a horizontal position, spread his arms out from side to side, and began to move them in a circular motion, faster and faster until his arms disappeared. By doing this, it caused him to be propelled in the direction he was facing, straight at Popobawa's neck.

The bat-winged monster saw Saka coming for it and looked him dead in the eye. Then Popobawa smiled as it caused a sonic boom by flapping its wings, picking up speed trying to get to Icya! Soon, another sonic boom rang out, then another. Now moving at breakneck speed, Saka was right on the tail of Popobawa. Saka yelled at the top of his lungs with his super voice, "Okay then!"

The power from his voice made Popobawa's wing ripple. Then there was another sonic boom as Saka slammed into the monster's neck and drove it deep into the forest floor. Both of them were underground for a minute until the ground started shaking and Popobawa crawled out of the dirt, squealing in pain and missing one wing.

A few seconds later, the ground started shaking again as Saka slowly emerged up from out of the earth with his head tilted to the side, walking on all fours like a gorilla. His whole body pulsated. Popobawa's body at this point was fully healed, and its missing wing had grown back. "Sooo full of passion and rage, Prince Saka. Well, she was a rather feisty beauty and also quite tasty," said Popobawa, growling and flapping its newly regenerated wing and walking towards Saka.

"Don't talk, die!" screamed Saka as he pulled out his sword and boomed towards the villainous monster, causing Popobawa to slash in his direction but come up short when Saka instantly changed direction and went around Popobawa, slicing through a tree. Quickly, Saka lunged at Popobawa with his sword, slashing and slashing at it in what seemed to be a fit of uncontrolled rage. Even with all the strength the amulet gave him, his sword had not pierced the flesh of Popobawa, so he started aiming for its eye. Bink, bink, bink, Saka's sword sounded off as he swung overhead, hitting the arm the monster used to guard its face. Then with incredible speed, Popobawa jumped in the air, causing Saka to miss and stumble forward. The beast then came down on Saka, grabbed him by the back and neck, lifted him up, and flew swiftly towards a huge tree.

Realizing that he was about to get banged into the base of the tree, Saka gripped his sword tightly and before he hit the tree, he sliced through it and upon impact was knocked loose from Popobawa's grip. Then, boom, Saka moved in a flash and began to slash through the large, tall trees, making a gigantic circle around the smelly beast. Now, the trees are starting to fall towards Popobawa, so it attempted to fly high over them, but Saka grabbed it by the legs and slammed it to the forest floor. Without delay, Saka moved out of the path of one of the falling trees as it crashed down on Popobawa's back. The powerful demon pushed the big tree off itself but, as soon as it stood up, Saka advanced down on it fast, batting it in that hideous set of razor- sharp teeth, shattering the majority of them, and sending it walloping back to the ground.

Meanwhile, the King, Icya and half of the Hazinan army were racing through the night forest on their way to Shetani, committed to the mission to kill or capture Congion. Thundar had already talked to his father, grabbed Volaris and doubled back to finish destroying the Nephlim. The other half of the army was with him. After riding for many hours at a demanding pace, the King ordered the men to stop and set up camp for a few hours. The sun was about to rise, and everyone, including the animals, needed to rest a little.

Back in the woods near the wood camp, Saka was still beating the crap out of Popobawa, but the murderous monster kept regenerating, so it was an ongoing recurring beatdown. At least that's what it seemed and was what Saka wanted Popobawa to believe.

During Prince Saka's years of schooling, he had learned about many creatures of fact and myth. Popobawa was one of them. Saka had read all about its transformation into a human body at dawn. He also knew that the Popobawa demon was more than just a simple possession of an ancient monster. It was fueled by the souls of a couple of legions granted to it by the ruler of hell himself. He was like the devil's brother on earth, and there was only one way to kill him.

The trees that Saka cut down had systematically formed somewhat of a cage around them, and his plan was in full effect. By now, Popobawa had realized what the Prince was trying to do so, at every turn, it was looking for a way to escape but, with every attempt, Saka pulverized it deeper into the forest floor.

At one point in this epic beatdown, Saka pinned the underworld general down on its back and with both hands clinched together, banged its arms and chest until both of them were twenty feet in the ground. Then he pulled its unconscious, broken and wingless body from underground and punched a hole into its eye out through the back of its head. After a few minutes, Popobawa had fully recovered and, in another futile attempt to flee, was brutally beaten for hours until it was time for it to die.

"Brother, are you done with the giant?" **asked** Saka.

"Yes, the men are taking its body parts out of the city and burning them as we speak," replied Thundar.

"Good, come give me a hand," said Saka.

"On my way," replied Thundar as he jetted off in Saka's direction. Saka had battered Popobawa so much that it was taking a lot longer for it to regenerate. Sitting on a large tree stump, Saka watched with his head slightly tilted as a crushed Popobawa stumbled away trying to regenerate and escape. Its neck and back were broken. It was really broken up now. Every step it took, it fell down on its half of face.

After about ten minutes, the fowl, one-eyed monster had almost recovered and the sun was about to come up. Popobawa was about to attempt to fly as Saka stood up, but before Saka could get to it, Thundar said, **"I got him!"** and came flipping out of the sky, landing precisely behind Popobawa. Popobawa was startled and even looked scared when Thundar grabbed both of its wrists from the back, roaring a sound that tore the wretched flesh off the side of its face. Then Thundar put his foot in the middle of the monster's back and began to pull and push until Popobawa's chest split right down the middle. Popobawa screeched in what sounded like the most dire pain imaginable.

"Oh, does that hurt? How dare you take my brother's hearrrrrt!" screamed Thundar as his foot went through the monster's body. Saka calmly walked close to them, pulling out the diamond-tipped blade that Zulin's father had given him.

"Okay then! Playtime's over, boy," said Saka, his head still tilted as the sun peeked over the tree and shined brightly on the big, bloodshot eye of Popobawa.

"So you think killing me will stop anything? Do you think killing Congion will stop what is coming? The seeds have been planted and, as long as you claim to be so-called guardians of the Incwadi Endala, you doom you and your family to a death worthy of hell's glory," said Popobawa.

The one-eyed, winged monster was just starting to change when Thundar put his hands inside its body, ripped it open wide, and watched as Saka raised the diamond-tipped dagger high above his head with tears in his eyes and jammed, then twisted the blade deep into Popobawa's eyeball. The fowl demon attempted to scream but, as soon as it opened its mouth, Thundar ripped its body in two and slammed each part ferociously to the ground, leaving the head at the end of Prince Saka's blade. Then all of a sudden, all the pieces of Popobawa's body, including the head, burst into flames.

"Okay, brother, we have to go now. Father is expecting us," said Thundar. Looking down at the blaze, Saka raised his head and said, "Let's go." Then, boom, they were gone in a flash.

Chapter XXVI

Weary Souls

Back deep in the Congolese Forest, north of Hazina, King O'Saka and Icya were sitting by a campfire talking. King O'Saka asked Icya why she was willing to kill her father. She told him that the man inside Shetani castle was not her father and she was quite sure that he could not be killed. They would have to trap and imprison him with a dangerous and powerful spell from the Dark Grimoires. The King also asked her how she got the book and from where. She lied and told him that she did not know how her father had gotten the book. She said she had stolen it from him after seeing the effects of its dark magic on her father and that the book was the reason Congion sent Popobawa to look for her.

King O'Saka then told her what had happened to Zulin. The horrible news hurt her deeply, and the tears began to pour down her face like the pour of the waterfalls of the Nile. Even though she and Zulin did not get along all the time, she still considered her a very close friend. This reaction threw the King for a loop, so he asked her why this hurt her so much when she did not know Zulin. Icya told him that she had met her at Saka's birthday celebration and that she could just imagine how terrible it must have been. But she said the main reason it pained her is that she knew how Saka must be feeling right now. She went on to explain that she had lost a loved one but left out a detail or two like the name of the deceased person and the fact that, in the beginning, she had been impersonating that person to spy on the King for her father.

A short time later, Saka and Thundar arrived outside the camp. Then they took off their amulets. As they walked inside the camp and through the ranks, all of the soldiers kneeled down and bowed their heads to honor the world's mightiest heroes.

When they came upon their father and Icya, she ran to Saka and embraced him, ensuring him that everything would be okay. Then without a second thought, she kissed him and they began to kiss each other until Saka realized what he was doing and gently pushed her away.

"Son, are you okay?" asked King O'Saka. "Yes, Father, I'm fine."

"So I take it it's done," inquired King O'Saka.

"Yes, what is the plan?" asked Saka. "Come, let's talk," replied the King as he grabbed Saka by the shoulder and beckoned to Thundar to come with them. They walked off to themselves along with General Nakatu.

"The young lady Icya told me she knows of some portals placed in the forest close to the Victoria River. The portals can get us inside Shetani very close to the house of Congion. The problem with the portals is that they are very narrow. Our forces on horse can go through only two, maybe three at a time. She also told me that she believes that her father Congion cannot be killed, but if you guys weaken him enough, she believes she can use a spell out of the Dark Grimoires to bind him long enough for us to lock him up and sink him to the bottom of Treazur Lake," explained King O'Saka.

"Sounds like a good plan to me, Father. I'm going to go take a catnap. I'm feeling a little tired," replied Saka in a weary voice as he walked over to his resting quarters, laid down and went to sleep. Thundar was not too far behind, for he was also very tired and desperately needed to rest.

A couple of hours passed and the time had come to march on Shetani. The king sent General Nakatu to wake the boys. When General Nakatu got to the tent, he called out to Saka but got no response, so he went inside and shook Thundar to try to wake him but could not. He tried for about ten minutes to break them from their deep slumber, but no matter how hard he shook them or how loud he yelled, they would not wake up. Hearing General Nakatu's loud yells, King O'Saka and Icya made their way to the boys' tent.

"What's going on?" asked the King as he walked into the tent.

"They won't wake up. I have tried to wake them for a while now, but no matter what I do to them, they won't respond," replied Master Nakatu, with a deep look of concern. Icya watched closely.

"They're not dead, are they?" asked the King as he nervously grabbed Prince Saka by the shoulders and shook him frantically. Then he put his head on the Prince's chest to see if he could hear his heartbeat. "Thank God, he's alive," said King O'Saka as he laid Saka back down and then listened to Thundar's chest.

"It must be the result of extended use of the amulets' magic without rest. They had never worn the amulets this long before. I'm sure they will be fine after a full day of rest," said General Nakatu.

"Okay, I pray you are right. Get some of the men, bring Volaris and carefully secure both the boys across her back. We have to leave now," said the King. So they secured the boys on Volaris, packed up everything and left.

Meanwhile, back in Shetani, Congion and his demented followers, Mama Yewande and Legion, were standing in front of Shetani castle preparing to ambush King O'Saka's forces. Congion did not have a massive army like King O'Saka. Therefore, he would have to pull off something that was evil, underhanded and conniving to ambush an army the size of the one on its way to his front doorstep.

"So how do you plan to defeat an army of such size and power? The boy has killed your monster Popobawa. Both the boy and the monkey have become more than a match for our meager manpower, and most of them have run off anyway," said Mama Yewande as she scowled at Congion.

"Shut up, woman! There is no reason to fear. This forest will not let me die. It wants the book here as much as I do! O'Saka, his monkey twins and his oversized army are en route to their own funeral. Yes. Come one, come all, the more the merrier, hahahaha," laughed Congion in a deep, demonic voice that sounded like multiple voices as he looked over Mama Yewande's head towards the dark, haunted forest. "It has all the power I will ever need," said Congion.

"What does?" questioned Yewande.

"This land, this forest is immersed in my kind of power.

Congion had known for a long time that the dark castle of Shetani was built in the center of a huge ancient burial ground. The people who rest there were once a great tribe of evil warriors that lived and ruled ten thousand years ago until the women of the tribe killed all of the males. Their mother's wives and daughters massacred husbands and sons. They poisoned their food to weaken them, then sliced their throats in their sleep with special blades given to them by a voodoo priestess. The women passed around one special blade and used it to kill hundreds of men and boys in one night. No one really knows why the women did what they did, but some people say they were drenched in cruelty, treated like slaves and forced to fight on the front lines in times of war. The men were said to have neither emotions nor compassion for the women or children, and their eyes were said to be as black as a crow's foot. The story goes on to say that they were not men at all, but demons. The women then were said to have fled Shetani and never seen again.

Two days had passed. Saka and Thundar were up walking around and feeling like their regular selves. They were about a day away from the Victoria River. It was late, so the King decided to stop to set up camp for a couple of hours.

Later that night, King O'Saka, General Nakatu, Saka and Thundar were sitting around a campfire, eating and conversing. Saka wasn't really saying much. King O'Saka noticed that Icya was a few feet away, sitting alone by a tree.

Saka and Icya had not said a word to each other since that ill-timed, awkwardly long and extremely passionate kiss that happened almost three days ago. Not even as much as a hello from either of them, they had barely even made eye contact. King O'Saka also noticed that Saka would look over in Icya's direction every so often.

"My son, go talk to her. Both of you are in unfamiliar territory in your lives right now. I know you are hurting, but maybe her conversation can cure your thoughts. She seemed to be a very nice and intelligent girl. Go ahead," said the King. Saka just sat there and looked at his father with a confused look in his eyes. Then he looked at Thundar and said, "No, I don't want to talk to anyone. No, you know who I want to talk to! Zulin! I want to talk to Zulin!" yelled Saka as he got up and began to walk away.

"Hold on, Saka. I am sorry. Maybe I said too much. Please sit down," said King O'Saka. Saka stopped and as he turned around, one of the guards was walking by him. Suddenly, the campfire blazed high, roaring in a purple and black inferno. Everyone ran away from the fire, but the guard was engulfed in a thick, black smoke that reached outward. Thundar ran to help the guard but was burned when he tried to pull him out of the demonic smoke. Now fearing they were helpless to prevent whatever was happening to the guard, everyone just watched as the black, wet smoke proceeded to go into the mouth of the poor, unfortunate man as he kicked and clawed at his throat. Icya was now hiding behind a tree as the man lay face down on the ground motionless and then without moving his arms or bending his knees, the guard stood straight up and turned towards the tree that Icya was hiding behind without moving his feet. Icya slowly crouched down and peeped from behind the tree.

At once, Saka and Thundar advanced towards the possessed guard, but King O'Saka told them to wait. Then the guard said in a hideous, gurgling voice, "Bring the book spells here, child, and spare the lives of everyone." Then strangely the expression on Icya's face changed from weak and afraid to confident and angry as she stood up and walked from behind the tree with her right arm outstretched and her palms in the guard's direction.

"What is your name, demon? Speak your name now!" she commanded. The demon inside the guard struggled to resist but could not.

"Trusron," replied the demon as his head started vibrating uncontrollably. "Arghh, all of you will die. Your great army will be the means to your glorious demise. Arghh!" screamed the demon-possessed guard.

"Leave this vessel now, I command you, Trusron! I send you back to hell from whence you came. Leave this world and never return again!" commanded Icya as the black, wet smoke started to pour from the guard's eyes, this time burning his eyesockets and blinding the poor soul. Screaming in agony, he fell to the ground, and the smoke went back into the fire and the fire's blaze went back to normal. With no hesitation, Icya ran to the man, got down on the ground with him, grabbed him in her arms, put her hands over his eyes, and started chanting under her breath.

When she stopped chanting and took her hand from over the man's eyes, they were back and just like new. Everyone was amazed at this beautiful young woman's power. As she got up, she gently laid the guard's head down on the ground for he was unconscious.

"Is he going to be okay?" asked Saka.

"Oh, you can talk now. Yes, he will be fine," replied Icya with a slightly tired and upset look on her face. Saka looked at Thundar and shrugged his shoulders, and Thundar did the same.

The next morning before the sun rose, King O'Saka lay deep in heavy thought in his tent, most likely thinking about what the demon had said before Icya exorcised it. He sat up, got on his knees and began to pray.

"Oh great God of my father and my father's father. I thank thee for waking me up this morning. I thank thee for my boys whom you have blessed with honest strength, love and wisdom, centuries beyond their youth. Honorable Yeshua, I thank thee for all things taken for granted and not within the time frame permitted to give thanks this morning. I come to you this morning asking oh Lord to guide me and mine on a journey to an evil, treacherous place. Give us the strength to carry out your will and do what is right in your name, Lord. You are an all-knowing and all-seeing powerful God. For your power has no equal.

"Help us Lord as we go to purge the world of a tormented soul who threatens to destroy the wonderful world and life that you have seen fit to bestow upon us. He aligns himself with the angel that was cast down for the unforgivable betrayal of your great kingdom. I do not know what evil mischief he has planned, and I know sacrifices must be made in the name of all that is right. Please Lord, I ask you to take into account the fact that we have already lost so many people who were dear to us, in the past and in the very recent present. Please protect us and lead us to absolute victory. We love you, Lord. In Yeshua's name I pray, amen," said the King as he got up and went outside.

Saka, Thundar, General Nakatu and Icya were waiting for him outside his tent, and he was just now rising up off his knees. The army was in perfect formation awaiting the king's orders. "Are you ready, sire?" asked Nakatu.

"Yes, my friend, let's go," he replied, looking over to Saka, Thundar and their newfound, old friend Icya.

The next night, they arrived at the first portal, went through and experienced firsthand the benefit and the pricey cost of using the portal presented. As expected, only three men on horses could pass through at one time. That was very time-consuming and would likely prove very dangerous once they reached Shetani. With all the King's men forced to funnel out of one small space, Congion's forces could concentrate their attack on that one area and considerably diminish numbers of the King's army with minimal effort. This fact left little room for a plan of attack. On the other hand, it would have taken weeks of travel and a lot more preparation to reach Shetani without the use of the portals. It took two hours for the army to pass through the first portal.

Chapter XXVII

Congion's Army

On their way to the northern portal, King O'Saka explained to the boys that they would have to pass through the portals first. Saka and Thundar were eager to do this. When they finally came upon the portal, Icya unsealed it. The boys had their amulets on and powered up, and they approached it with no fear but entered with caution. Thundar went first, then Saka. Inside, the portal was quite dark but at the same time strangely lit, like having your eyes closed facing a bright and vibrant sun. A damp, sweet, husky fume was heavy in the nostrils and eyes. There was also the sound of a deep moaning almost as if the tree was breathing. When they came out of the other side, to their surprise everything was quiet and no one was in sight. They walked farther out into the forest but not a sound could be heard, not even the wildlife.

"Why so quiet?" asked Thundar.

"Don't know, but I do know we will find out soon enough," replied Saka as he walked back through the portal to report to his father the status of the other side. It took a while, but eventually the entire army was on the other side of the portal in formation. Then King O'Saka gave the command, and they began the march on Shetani.

As the army advanced towards the dark castle, the King, Saka, Thundar and Icya dropped back to the massive regiment. After a while, it began to thunder and lightning. The closer they got to the castle, the more severe the weather became. The lightning began to stretch from the heavens and strike the ground directly in front of the dark castle, hitting trees and starting fires.

What was once a light drizzle turned into a drastic downpour of heavy rain and roaring winds. The path under the regiment's feet was turning into a dangerously slippery mess. Now the army was right in front of Shetani castle. King O'Saka told General Nakatu to give the order to stop. As soon as the army stopped, King O'Saka looked to his right side at Thundar and nodded his head.

Thundar then got down off Volaris into the water and mud, jumped fifty feet in the air, and with his super voice said, "Congion, I am Prince Thundar of the kingdom Hazina, son of King O'Saka Navitazi. Come forth and surrender, or we will come get you by force with extreme prejudice. You have thirty minutes to comply." Then he descended back to the ground, landing on the side of Volaris with a big splash.

Meanwhile, deep inside the castle in the room where Icya had witnessed the evil ceremony, Congion, Mama Yewande and Yejide were sitting in a circle around a large, black fire with purple smoke pulsating from it. As the smoke filled the room and went out and up the stairs, the four evildoers' eyes rolled back in their heads while they chanted ancient words repeatedly.

The room was dark and freezing, even though there candles burning everywhere and, again, a large purple inferno was blazing. All that could be seen in the circle was the purple fire, their eyes glowing red, and the frost coming from their mouths going downward into the ground instead of up. Twenty minutes had passed, and it was still raining and storming like crazy, until all of a sudden, the rain stopped and everything went quiet again. Then the front door opened on the castle. It was Legion, with his fiery skull and a long trail of black smoke that stretched from his back all the way back to the dungeon. He walked out of the doors and said, "Send the girl and the book of spells and leave this place or all of you will die tonight." Then, boom, Thundar blasted off and in a millisecond was standing right in front of Legion.

"Now, you and what army are supposed to be issuing all of these death certificates?" asked Thundar as he looked down on Legion's flaming, hot head.

Legion nonchalantly looked up at him and said, "Yours." Then all of a sudden, FABOOOOM, Legion's body exploded in an enormous red, black and purple cloud of smoke, sending Thundar flying hundrededs of feet through the air. He landed in almost the same spot where he was before. Luckily, Saka ran and caught him before he hit the ground.

"Wow, what was that?" asked Saka as he put his brother down.

"Don't know, but could you tell me why all the men are turned towards us? Look at their eyes," said Thundar as he turned three hundred and sixty degrees and scanned his surroundings. All the men's eyes were black as coal; even King O'Saka was now possessed. Quickly, Icya reached her hand out towards the King and began to exorcise the demon from the King's body.

Now the demon-filled men were running towards Icya and the King, but before they could get to them, Saka and Thundar were knocking them all over the place.

"Thundar, try not to hurt them. These are our people," said Saka as he circled Icya and his father, pushing the men back onto each other and causing a pileup.

"I know, brother," replied Thundar as he tossed the advancing soldiers on top of the rising pile.

Meanwhile, Icya has exorcised the demons from King O'Saka and General Nakatu. "How long will the men be in this condition? Can you help them, Icya, like you helped us?" asked King O'Saka as he slapped one of the men with the handle of his sword.

"There are too many of them. The only one who can stop this madness is my father."

"Boys, clear a path so …," said the King, but before he could finish his sentence, he found himself inside the castle, standing on Icya's bed.

"Sorry about that, King O'Saka. I did not mean to startle you. This is my room, well, my old room. I will never call this place home again," whispered Icya as she, the King and General Nakatu stepped down off the bed. The room was dark and very cold.

"What about the boys?" whispered the king. "They'll be fine," replied the general.

"Come on, let's go," whispered Icya as she opened the door a little to peep and see what she could see. Then they left the room and went into the hallway, making their way towards the dungeon. The hallway was lit up with torches but still bone-numbing cold. King O'Saka grabbed one of the torches. They had taken about ten steps when General Nakatu stopped and said, "Something's wrong. I cannot move. Then a gust of wind blew out all the torches. Icya snapped her fingers, and the torch King O'Saka was holding begin to burn again.

Straining and trying to move, General Nakatu picked his head up toward the ceiling and to his surprise he saw Apunda hovering high above them with demon-filled eyes. Then Apunda with the flick of her wrist sent him crashing into the wall, knocking his sphere out of his hand and almost rendering him unconscious. Quickly, King O'Saka ran over to him and helped him up.

"Come down from there, Apunda. Where are your manners?" said Icya as she looked up at Apunda with a crooked smile and her head tilted. Suddenly, Apunda fell from the ceiling and landed on her feet.

"Icya, you've come home to us. We've missed you so," said Apunda, standing in the middle of the hallway with her hand on her hip and licking her lips.

"Oh, is that so? Where is Congion, Apunda?" asked Icya as she walked a little closer to Apunda.

"They left for the party," replied Apunda with a big, fat smirk on her face.

"Tell me where they are or I'm going to wipe that big, fat smirk right off your face."

"Do it! Hahaha! Am I supposed to be scared of ...," screamed Apunda, but before she could finish the rest of her sentence, her mouth had disappeared. Then as Icya walked all the way up on Apunda, she calmly chanted a spell that paralyzed Apunda and left her helpless, just standing there and moving her mouthless head.

Now standing on the side of Apunda with her nose touching Apunda's right ear, Icya whispered, "How does it feel, sister? Now I am going to ask you one more time. Where is father? Apunda strained to turn her head towards Icya and then attempted to spit, but instead snot shot out of her nose onto Icya's face. Icya backed up, wiped her face with her forearm, and started chanting a spell that shrunk Apunda's head down to the size of an apple. As Icya walked away from Apunda, she said to General Nakatu in a calm voice, "Kill her."

General Nakatu looked at King O'Saka and said, "Who died and made her boss?"

King O'Saka looked at the shrunken-headed evil twin, then looked back at Nakatu and said, "What are you waiting for?"

Then without any hesitation, Nakatu thrust his sphere through Apunda's heart, pulled it back out, and walked away with the King as the body of one of the evil twins fell to the ground.

Back on the battlefield, Saka and Thundar had decided to try even harder not to hurt their demon-possessed countrymen, so they have let them back deep into the forest and hidden from them high atop an enormous tree.

"Do you think one of us should go and check on father?" asked Thundar as he looked down at the men scrambling around looking for them.

"No, they are okay. I can hear them," replied Saka, staring off into the trees as he used his super abilities to listen in on his father and the rest of them.

"You can hear them from here? Impressive," said Thundar.

"Thanks, brother. It's easy. I'll show you how to do it," replied the Prince. Then suddenly the tree they were atop started to shake and then tilt as the men began to chop it down and shoot arrows at them. "Okay then! Time to go," said Saka as he and Thundar jumped to another tree and hid.

Back in the dark castle, Icya and the rest of them were making their way to the dungeon, where she suspected her father and the rest of his followers were. As Icya led them down the dark hallway, the King and General Nakatu followed behind her, watching as she displayed almost no fear, moving apace through the darkness as if she was on a righteous crusade.

"She is a lot stronger than she appears, wouldn't you say, Nakatu," whispered the king.

"Yes, sire. It's a little scary, I might add," replied Nakatu as they came upon the stair leading to the dungeon. "Icya, Icya," whispered the King. "Where are we going?" he asked.

"The dungeon, where he does most of his evil," she replied as they walked down the stairs. The farther they got down the stairwell, Icya noticed that there was no light coming from the dungeon. No candles or torches were burning, and it was really quiet. When they reached the bottom of the stairs and entered the dungeon, Icya said, "Be careful. I know they are here." But as she turned around to look at them, Mama Yewande was staring back at her, holding the torch that General Nakatu was holding, and she said, "I am right here, my dear." Then bam! Mama Yewande hit Icya over the head with the torch and knocked her unconscious. "Stupid, backstabbing child! Where is the book, girl?" asked Mama Yewande as she searched Icya up and down and side to side.

Meanwhile back in the forest, Saka can hear that something was wrong inside the castle. By now, they had led the demon-possessed army a great distance away from the dark abode and more importantly away from their father. **Brother, something is wrong. I have to go now,"** said Saka as he jumped down and blasted off in a sonic boom, heading for the house of Congion. Standing on a branch atop a very tall tree, Thundar watched his brother as he blazed toward the castle. Then as he glanced over the blanket of crazed demonic vessels, a curious look came upon his face and then a smile.

Back deep inside in the castle, Icya still lay unconscious on the cold, hard floor in a puddle of her own blood. Mama Yewande had been gone for a while but was now back to retrieve her. She bent down, grabbed Icya by the arms, and dragged her deep into the dungeon and into darkness. "Oh my goodness, you have gained weight," said Mama Yewande as she struggled to drag Icya.

"Bring her to me," said Congion, and he walked farther in the darkness.

"I'm coming," replied Mama Yewande as she made her way to him. King O'Saka and General Nakatu lay not too far away, either unconscious or dead. Now standing over Icya, Congion knelt down and reached out his shiny, black hand, touching Icya's face. "Where is the book, my child?" asked Congion as his eyes rolled back in his head. Slowly, Icya regained consciousness and tried to push his hand away from her, but before she can, he let her go and said, "You don't have to tell me. I know where it is now. Legion, go and retrieve the Dark Grimoires from inside the north portal.

Deep in the forest, Legion has possessed the body of one of the soldiers. He has been cautiously watching Thundar's every move, alerting his demons to his whereabouts. With Thundar's back towards him, he carefully summoned some of the demons out of about ten soldiers into the body he possessed, then he heeded to his master's command, hopped on a horse and began racing towards the north portal. Now, the unpossessed men were in the middle of all the possessed men. Luckily, they were all trying to find Thundar and kill him, so the possessed vessel soldier had not noticed them yet.

Chapter XXVIII

All Too Familiar

Meanwhile back at the Shetani castle, Saka had made it inside and was now at the bottom of the stairwell. He could see King O'Saka and General Nakatu tied and gagged in the floor about twenty feet in front of him. Swiftly he ran to them, but abruptly fell into a big hole in the floor and was impaled through his chest by a huge diamond shard. Prince Saka was hurt very badly and could not remove himself from the large diamond. There were also diamond shards sticking up from the floor, now piercing through the Prince's feet.

This dungeon was a smaller version of the training cavern back in Hazina. It was full of diamonds in the wall and under the ground. From out of the darkness, Congion and Mama Yewande appeared with Icya tied and gagged, barely conscious. Now standing over Saka, Congion looked down at him, then looked back up at Mama Yewande and said, "Now do you see, a grave fitting a Prince. So eager to save his loved one! This incorrect perception on invulnerability has clouded the judgment of the boy. Now he is the one in dire straits. I know everything there is to know about the power you now have so recently acquired, and the one weakness. Why do you think I have gone through all the formalities to possess the Dark Grimoires? It is the question and the answer to all that is relevant in this world and the next." Saka looked up at him and tried to pull himself up off the diamond shard but could not.

"Wake up, O'Saka," said Congion as he stretched his hands out towards the king. Suddenly, King O'Saka awakened, screaming in pain from whatever Congion was causing to happen. "Look, O'Saka, look there at your boy, isn't this all too familiar?"

"Saka, Saka, where are you, son?" said the King, half out of it.

"Oh, that's right, you can't see him. Here let me help you," said Congion as he walked over to the King, picked him up by the back of his neck, yanked the cloth from his eyes, walked over to the big hole, and dangled him over it. "Dear Nidera perished in a similar fashion, didn't she, old friend?" said Congion.

"I did not give you the book because I knew it would do this to you. It is evil, and you have allowed it to consume you with that evil. Hold on son," said King O'Saka. Then Prince Saka picked up his head a little, looked at his father, smiled and said, "Brother." Now all of them could hear and feel a loud roar that got louder and stronger by the second. It was Thundar and he was frantically pulsating with anger.

When he got to the stairwell, he just jumped down, still roaring with his super voice, knocking everyone down to the ground except Congion. Thundar's angry eyes scanned over the dungeon searching for Saka until he saw him half-dead in the pit. With not a second thought, he jumped down to his brother.

"Ahrrrrrr," roared Thundar, as the diamond shards pierced both of his feet. Icya was now fully awake and chanting a spell that turned the legs of Mama Yewande into snake legs. Mama

Yewande slipped down and hit her head on the hard black ground, and then Icya shoved her into the diamond shard pit to her inevitable demise.

"Brother, help me," said Saka, gurgling in his own blood and reaching out to Thundar. Using every bit of his will, he finally made it to his brother and grabbed ahold of him, trying to push Saka up off the large shard protruding upward out of his back. With every push upward to save his brother, his feet were pushed downward and a smaller shard pushed up through his feet into his legs, but that would not stop him.

Meanwhile, Icya had untied General Nakatu, who was searching for a rope or something to pull the boys out of the hole. She also told him that Congion had read her mind and discovered the whereabouts of the Dark Grimoires, and subsequently had sent one of his flunkies to retrieve it from the north portal. Congion seemed to be in a trance as he knelt down near the pit holding the bound and gagged King O'Saka, helpless to save his son. Until then, out of nowhere, he let him go. At that same instant, Thundar pushed Saka completely off the shard and threw him out of the hole. King O'Saka hopped up and ran to Saka, while General Nakatu helped Thundar pull himself up out of the pit with an old rope he had found.

Icya was now standing over her father chanting a spell. Saka had regained his strength and with haste pounced on top of Congion and began to pulverize him into the ground. As soon as Thundar got out of the hole and healed, he joined his brother. They beat him until he was just a splattered mess of blood, skin and bones.

After satisfying their rage, they stopped and went to their father to make sure he was okay, but as soon as they turned their backs, a naked Congion reappeared in the place of the bloody pile. Congion just stood there staring at Icya with his demon-filled eyes. Icya had never stopped chanting. She had memorized and was using one of the spells she had learned in the Dark Grimoires. It prohibited Congion from moving or using magic to do harm to anyone.

"Can you keep this up until we reach Ardhi Anasa? I have an idea how we can free the men from the demons that possess them," said Saka. She nodded her head yes, and Saka wrapped Congion with his torn clothes. He then grabbed Congion, picked him up and put him over his shoulder. On the way out of the castle, General Nakatu remembered what Icya had told him, so he told everyone else. As soon as Thundar heard what he had to say, he jetted off in a boom to intercept the demon trying to retrieve the Dark Grimoires.

When the rest of them made it outside, they could see all the demon-possessed men in the distance, now fighting one another. "Here brother, hold him for a while," said Prince Saka as he handed Congion over to General Nakatu. He then ran and jumped hundreds of feet into the air over the possessed men and, in his super voice, began chanting word for word, the same exorcising phrases that had expelled the demons from King O'Saka and General Nakatu earlier. Looking up at Saka, the demon-filled men appeared confused and afraid. As Saka descended rapidly, continuously chanting louder and louder, a thick, black, leathery cloud of smoke filled the air above the men. Then as Saka came thundering down upon the forest floor, causing the demon cloud to disperse, a new and most saddening vantage point revealed itself.

Now Prince Saka could see the hundreds of men who had died by the hand of their possessed brothers in arms. Severed heads, arms and legs lay scattered far and near. Saka looked around for a minute or two, then with a heavy heart he dropped to his knees and began to weep loudly.

In the meantime, King O'Saka, Icya and General Nakatu came upon Saka's position. "Are you alright, my son?" asked the King as he put his hand on Saka's wide shoulders but at the same time surveyed the horrid sight that now circled him.

"I'm fine, Father," said Saka as he stood up wiping his eyes. Icya looked at Saka with intense sadness in her eyes that soon turned into pure rage when she set her gaze upon her father. The whole time she maintained the incantation that imprisoned Congion's mind and body.

"Father," said Saka.

"Yes, what is it son?" replied King O'Saka.

"Thundar has the book. I should take Icya and Congion to the place we discussed and continue with our plans. I will meet brother there. Icya looks tired. I don't know how long she can keep up the incantation," said Prince Saka as he took Congion from General Nakatu and slammed him over his shoulder.

"You are right. Go now and do what must be done," said King O'Saka as he whistled for Zolatar and Volaris.

"Come, Icya, let's go," said Saka, holding out his hand to her. At first, she looked at him nervously for a while, but slowly she extended her hand out to his, quickly took two steps, then a high leap and straddled her legs around his waist with her arms around his chest. Saka then put his free arm tightly around her, took a few steps away from his father, and boooom, he took off for Ardhi Anasa.

Chapter XIX

Treazur Lake Part Two

When they passed through the first portal, Saka stopped and asked Icya if she was okay. Her hair was all over her head, and she was a little taken aback by the speed and pure power of the Prince, but she looked up at him, smiled and said, "Yes, my Prince." Then they took off again. When they got to Ardhi Anasa, Thundar was waiting on them at Treazur Lake with the Dark Grimoires and a large, black chest.

Now standing on the banks of the lake, Saka gently put Icya down. She could barely stand. He then took Congion down off his shoulders, turned him around, slammed him to the ground, and plunged his big foot into the back of his head, pressing it firmly into the sand.

"Saka, we have to hurry," said Icya as she repeatedly chanted a spell. "I cannot keep him under for much longer."

"Thundar, hurry, help me find something to bind this fool," said Saka. Thundar leaped into the trees, retrieved some strong vines, and brought them to the Prince. "This will have to do," said Saka. Then they tied Congion's hands and feet and threw him inside the chest.

"Please, he's coming to!" screamed Icya. Saka quickly closed the chest and locked it. Suddenly, the chest began to shake uncontrollably. "Ahhhhh," screamed Icya, holding her head with tears in her eyes as they rolled back in her head and veins popped out from her neck. "He's awake!" she yelled.

"Now brother, drag him to the deepest, darkest part of the lake, so that he may never rise again," said Saka. Thundar then grabbed the heavy chest with both hands and raised it over his head. He jumped at least twenty feet toward the middle of the lake and went in head-first. The air inside the chest pulled against him, but he was very strong and swam onward, descending ever so deep into Treazur Lake. Congion tried to scream, but the cursed water had already begun to eat away at his skin and, eventually, a mere skeleton remained.

Thundar soon came upon the bottom of the dark abyss and began to tie the chest to a large, smooth rock. As he tied the last knot around the giant gem, the rope was snatched out of his hand and now the chest was shaking again as if the corpse had come back to life. He swiftly secured the chest and looked inside a small hole.

"**Saka, I wish you could see this**," said Thundar. To his surprise, the corpse was fully restored to its former likeness and dreadfully reliving his previous horrible death. "**Serves him right for what he has done**," said Thundar as he swam back towards the surface.

About fifty feet above Thundar, at a reasonably safe distance from the lake,

Prince Saka and Icya anxiously waited for him to emerge.

"Is he okay?" asked Icya.

"He's fine. There he is," said Prince Saka.

"Rhaaaarhh, it's done brother," roared Thundar as he propelled fifteen feet into the air from the surface of the lake and landed two feet in front of Prince Saka.

"Thank the Lord you are safe," said Icya as she fainted into Prince Saka's arms, thoroughly exhausted from the hours spent in the incantation that kept Congion subdued.

"Okay then," said Saka as he picked up Icya and held her in his arms like a sleeping infant.

"It's okay, brother. Go let her rest. You could use some, too. I will go make sure Father and the others make it home safely. I will be back in a couple of days," said Thundar.

"Okay then brother, I'll see you soon," replied Saka as he turned around and walked towards the palace, carrying the sleeping Icya.

A couple of days passed. One rainy morning about three hours before sunrise, the King, Thundar, General Nakatu and the rest of the men were breaking down their camp and preparing to start their journey home. It was still fairly dark, and Thundar could hear someone coming towards them, breathing heavily. He quickly pounced down right in front of the intruder. It was a woman with torn clothing, covered in blood from her head to her toes. Thundar quickly caught her before she collapsed to the forest floor. "Father!" he yelled. King O'Saka quickly ran over to see what was going on.

"What is it, Thundar?" he asked as he looked and saw for himself. "Oh my goodness! Is she alive?" he asked.

"Barely," replied Thundar.

"Bring her to my tent," said King O'Saka. Thundar brought her to the King's tent and laid her down to let her rest a bit. Before the woman fell into a deep sleep, King O'Saka asked her, "My dear, what is your name?" The woman replied," My name is Sazi."

THE END

Epilogue

Meanwhile, high upon the mountainside of the tallest mountains in Africa (the Kilimanjaro), in a well-built hut filled with lit candles, a pregnant woman is showing signs of imminent labor. Lying on the floor of the hut, she screams in agony. For an hour she screams, floating in and out of consciousness until, in the middle of a silent, powerful push, a baby boy pokes his tiny, little head out of her womb and then plops down to the floor, kicking and crying. Panting franticly and soaked in sweat, the woman leans over and picks up the newborn and embraces him like any loving mother would.

They lay there for an hour. The baby has adjusted to his new habitat and has stopped crying for the moment. Then the woman grabs her stomach in pain and begins to scream again. Outside, the wind howls and the rain has started to come down heavily. It is about an hour before sunset, and the wiping winds have penetrated the drapes on the hut's doorway and blown out the candles. Now, it is dark inside the hut.

The woman screams continuously for thirty minutes straight until finally another small wonder pushes its way out into the world. It is another boy. The new mother of two big healthy identical twin boys grabs them and holds them tightly. She then puts them up to her breast and feeds them.

A few minutes pass, and the moon is just starting to peek over the mountaintop, when the woman sits up and places the newborn twins in the corner and says," Show me." The babies begin to yelp a terrible scream, both of their bodies began to float in midair, and an all-too-familiar transformation occurs, wings and all. "HAHAHA! You will grow big and strong, and I will teach you the ways of my father and, when the time is right, we will avenge my mother, beloved sister and your father. HAHAHA!" laughs Yejide.

A few special requests, after the movie script is made:

1. I would like former President Barack Obama to play the part of King O'Saka Navitazi.

2. I would like former First Lady Michelle Obama to play the part of Queen Nidera Navitazi.

3. I would like Sade to create the soundtrack, and I would like to do one song with her.

4. I would like Ariana Miyamoto to play the part of Zulin Yang.

Here are a few questions.

1. Who would be a great fit for the role of Prince Saka? Maybe (Bryshere Y. Gray)

2. Who would be a great fit for the role of Icya?

3. Had you forgotten about Sazi?

Visit www.darkGrimoires.com to answer questions and blog.

Back to TOP